Diana Hamilton

CLAIMING HIS WIFE

LATIN LOVERS

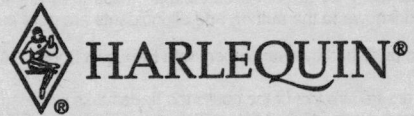

HARLEQUIN®

TORONTO • NEW YORK • LONDON
AMSTERDAM • PARIS • SYDNEY • HAMBURG
STOCKHOLM • ATHENS • TOKYO • MILAN • MADRID
PRAGUE • WARSAW • BUDAPEST • AUCKLAND

ISBN 0-373-12178-4

CLAIMING HIS WIFE

First North American Publication 2001.

Copyright © 2001 by Diana Hamilton.

This edition published by arrangement with Harlequin Books S.A.

Visit us at www.eHarlequin.com

Printed in U.S.A.

CHAPTER ONE

IT WAS warm and airless in the room, but not unbearably so. Outside on the bleached rolling miles of the *campos*, the heat of this July afternoon would be almost intolerable.

Cassie waited. Her body felt damp with perspiration beneath the grey and cream linen suit she had worn for the journey from London to the vast ·Las Colinas Verdes estates in Andalusia.

The suit, understatedly elegant and deliberately so, had survived the flight and the taxi-ride out here well, she thought thankfully. No way had she wanted to present herself looking less than businesslike and in control.

She lifted a hand to check that her rich chestnut hair was tamed, severely anchored into the nape of her neck. And her heartbeats were steady—that was another consolation. There was no reason for them to be otherwise, of course; she was no longer a nervous, besotted bride of just twenty-one. She was three years older and a whole lot wiser.

Satisfied that her appearance was as good as it could get—given her average kind of looks—she glanced at her watch and wondered how much longer she would have to wait. The taxi that had brought her from Jerez airport had deposited her here at the farmhouse over half an hour ago. The atmosphere in the heavily furnished, sombre room was beginning to stifle her, the louvres closed to keep out the merciless white heat of the sun.

'I will send someone to tell your husband that you are here,' her mother-in-law had stated. Doña Elvira had spoken politely; she always had, Cassie remembered, even when offering up her barbed insults, insults unfailingly echoed by her two older sisters, Roman's aunts—Tía Agueda and Tía Carmela.

'Is my son expecting you?' A faint pinching of patrician nostrils had denoted that that lady had known Roman was not, that he had long since lost whatever interest he might once have had in his unsuitable, estranged wife.

No longer as frighteningly squashable as she once had been, Cassie had ignored the question and coolly stated, 'I'll wait. In the meantime, I'd like to see Roy. Perhaps you could send him to me.'

And so she waited. Her disgraced twin brother, Roy, it transpired, was not available. He had been put to work erecting fences out on the estate, under the blistering sun, a part of the punishment that was only just beginning.

'I'm under house arrest at Las Colinas Verdes, while Roman decides what to do with me,' he'd complained during his distraught phone call of a couple of days ago. 'I can't face ten years in a Spanish jail, sis—I'd rather top myself!' he'd added, his voice beginning to rise with panic. 'You could persuade

Roman not to bring charges. He won't listen to me.
You know what he's like—he's got a tongue like a
whip and a mind like a maze; you never know what
he's thinking! It makes it impossible to get through
to him!'

'I'll phone him this evening,' Cassie had reluctantly promised. She'd felt sick with disappointment
over what her brother had done, the way he was
dragging her into the mess he had made. 'I'll call
him from the flat; the boutique's busy right now.' In
fact, it was buzzing with bargain-hunters on the first
day of their summer sale. Her boss and best friend,
Cindy Corfield, had already gestured frantically to
her to end this call and come up front to help out.
'Though Roman isn't likely to listen to me, either,'
she'd warned Roy, her voice tight. 'If I ask him not
to bring charges against you, he'll probably do just
the opposite to spite me. You shouldn't have been
such a damn fool in the first place!'

'I know, and I'm sorry—but for pity's sake, sis,
phoning him won't help me! He'd just hang up on
you—he's rigid with pride, you know that! Come out
here. He won't be able to blank you then. He'll listen
to you—well, he'll have to, won't he? Damn it all,
Cass, the guy's still in love with you, even if you did
walk out on him!'

Which was absurd. Roman Fernandez had *never*
loved her. He'd married her because it had been, for
him, a matter of expediency at the time. And for her?
She didn't think about that, not ever. Three years ago
she'd been naive and terribly vulnerable. Roman had

taken the tears from her eyes and replaced them with the stars that hadn't lasted much longer than the actual wedding ceremony.

But she was a mature adult now and refused to dwell on past mistakes. And because she'd looked out for her volatile twin for most of her life she'd agreed to do as he'd begged. Roy probably didn't deserve it, but she knew how frightened and alone he'd be feeling, so she'd give it her best shot and hope it would be good enough.

And so now she waited and refused to let herself fidget. During the forty-eight hours or so since she'd received her brother's cry for help she'd worked out what she would offer in return for Roy's freedom.

Offers only a hard-hearted brute could dismiss. She tried not to remind herself that that was exactly what Roman was, and against all her hopes and expectations her stomach flipped over when he finally walked into the room and closed the heavy panelled door behind him.

He was wearing a straight-brimmed black hat tipped forward over his eyes and the black denim of his shirt and jeans was covered in the dust of the *campos*. He brought the evocative scent of leather and maleness and white heat into the musty room that she knew from her long, lonely months spent here was never used, except as a repository for unwanted furniture.

She had never tried to pretend that he wasn't the most shatteringly fantastic-looking man she had ever seen, because that would have been pointless. But hoping she looked in control, like a woman who had taken a long hard look at her life, edited out all the bad bits—in which he featured as the central character—and got on with her life, she dismissed the impact he made.

Reminding herself that looks counted for nothing if they hid a hard, unloving heart, she rose to her feet. Five feet five inches of severely groomed adult woman, supported by three-inch spindly heels, was a match for any man, even if he was six feet something of steel-hard muscle and twelve years her senior.

'They told me you were here,' Roman imparted in the husky, sexily accented voice that, despite everything, still had the power to send shivers careering up and down her spine. 'I'm sorry to have kept you waiting.' He removed his hat, and sent it languidly spinning across the room to land on a dour-looking table beneath one of the shuttered windows, revealing slightly overlong soft hair, as dark as the wing of a raven, and smoky charcoal-grey eyes that told her he wasn't sorry at all.

Roman had never considered her feelings when they'd lived together. There was no reason on earth why he should do so now.

'So, what brings you?' He tilted his head in enquiry, his ruthless, sensual mouth unsmiling, his dark eyes cold. 'A year away, working in a second-rate dress shop in a little town that no one has ever heard of, living in a tiny, squalid flat above the premises, has made you wake up to the fact that you're far better off with your husband? Is that it?'

His long legs were straddled, his thumbs hooked into the waistband of his jeans, his unforgettable features blanking out whatever thoughts were passing through his cold, cruel mind.

She didn't want to look at him, but couldn't avoid it without appearing to be a coward or, worse, shifty, as if she had something despicable to hide. And the burn of inner heat that pulsed so violently through her veins was anger, nothing else.

Anger at his sarcastic denigration of her work, her home, the bitter knowledge that he must have kept tabs on her over the past twelve months without her being aware of it.

Not willing to waste breath on telling him that the boutique she ran with Cindy was thriving, that the flat above the premises might be small but was light years away from being squalid, she made her features as cool and unreadable as his and told him, 'I came because Roy's in trouble and he needs me.'

'Now, I wonder why that fails to surprise me.' The words were drawled, casually sardonic, but a flicker of some dark emotion over his harshly beautiful features and the thinning of his aristocratic nostrils told her she had somehow hit a nerve.

She narrowed her tawny eyes at him, waiting for some further reaction, something she might be able to use to her advantage. And when none came, and there was nothing but the thick, uncomfortable silence, she returned to the straight-backed heavily carved chair and lowered herself into its unforgiving embrace.

Slowly, she crossed her long silk-clad legs and watched him watching the unconsciously elegant, vaguely provocative movement; she realised with a tiny shock that made her breath catch in her lungs that his brooding eyes had taken in the way her narrow skirt had ridden way above her knees and quite definitely liked what they saw.

Sex. She would not let herself think about that.

She said levelly, refusing to let him see how nervous she had suddenly become, 'I understand how angry you must be with Roy. I feel exactly the same. What he did was nothing short of disgraceful.'

'Then for once in our lives, *mi esposa*, we are in agreement.'

Smooth, cool, even very faintly amused, his riposte didn't help. Twisting her fingers together, she pulled in a breath. 'But sending him to prison wouldn't help; you must see that. It would blight the rest of his life—he is only twenty-four...and *do* remember the hallowed Fernandez name.'

A bite in her voice there. She hadn't been able to help it. Pride in their exalted ancestry, the ownership of vast tracts of land supporting vines, cattle, wheat and olives, their place in society as members of one of the old sherry families, had been the favourite, seemingly endless topic of conversation between Doña Elvira and the aunts. Indulged in, she had no doubt at all about it, to reinforce their opinion that she was nowhere near good enough to be the wife of the heir to the kingdom!

'You are suggesting that his crime goes unpunished?'

Roman was moving now, with the indolent grace that was so characteristic of him, his wide hard shoulders relaxed, his lean body tapering down to flat, narrow hips and endless legs. He opened the louvres, letting the harsh light flood the room. Probably the better to see her, she thought tiredly.

He stood with his back to the windows, his face shadowed. Enigmatic. So what else was new? She had never been able to tell what he was thinking.

But that didn't matter. He was nothing to her now. She had walked out on their empty marriage a year ago and after another year she could begin divorce proceedings. All she cared about was helping her brother out of this mess and then getting back to England.

'If you don't bring charges against him, I'll take him back home with me—that could be a condition.' She offered the solution she had been turning over in her mind ever since Roy had phoned her. 'Leaving Spain permanently would be punishment enough. He loves this country.'

'I don't think so,' Roman replied implacably. 'What he loves about Spain is being connected by your marriage to one of the wealthiest families in Andalusia. It makes him feel important.'

Cynic! Cassie swallowed the instinctive accusation. Why waste her time and her breath on stating the obvious? He had married her for purely cynical reasons and nothing had changed.

Grimly, she refused to let memories eat away at the poise she had gathered during her year away from her unloving husband and his incurably snobbish family. She was over whatever it was that she had once felt for him and was making a life for herself where she was respected and liked, and where no one tried to make her feel inferior.

She straightened her already rigid shoulders, mentally crossed her fingers, and played her ace. 'Do you really want that sort of blot on the revered family name? Somehow, I don't think so. Imagine the gossip when it becomes known that Roman Fernandez's brother-in-law is behind bars.'

He moved into her line of vision, standing over her, his height, his breadth, the power of him suddenly and unwelcomingly intimidating.

'The sympathy would all be with my family for its association with yours. We would be seen as upholding the rule of law, no matter what the cost. Quite noble, you must agree.' He smiled, but his eyes were still cold and hard. 'You will have to do better than that.'

Cassie muffled a sigh and reined back the urge to slap that beautiful, arrogant face. There was no point in appealing to his better nature. Still less point in trying to get through to him. She had never been able to do that, not even when they were first married.

'I'll repay every peseta he stole from you,' she offered without a great deal of hope. She had no idea how much that was—Roy, to put it mildly, had been incoherent on that subject. It could take her the rest of her life, but it would be worth it. She lifted eyes to him that were now sparkling with defiance—she refused to admit that the emotion raging inside her was hurt—and said, 'You'll get your money back, get me and Roy out of your sight. In a year we can divorce and you can forget your precious family was ever associated with mine! And then—' she drew in a breath, surprised by the pain that gripped her heart in a cruel vice '—you can marry that highly suitable Delfina who was always hanging around. Make your mother and the aunts happy—Delfina, too. The way she flirted with you, and the way you played up to her, used to make me sick!'

Too late, she deeply regretted the unguarded words that had revealed some of those earlier painful insecurities. She was over them now; she didn't care who he eventually married. But his ego was too large to let him believe that simple fact, as was clearly demonstrated by the upward drift of one dark brow, the knowing tilt of his head.

He thought she was jealous, that she still felt something for him. It was intolerable!

Cassie shot to her feet, smoothing the non-existent wrinkles out of her skirt with unsteady hands. She was beginning to get a headache and her stomach was tying itself in tense knots because, so far, her visit hadn't achieved a thing except to remind herself of two of the most unhappy years of her life.

Still, she had to try. She tilted her chin. 'Do we have a deal?'

She couldn't plead with him, not even for her twin's sake. She had pleaded with Roman too often in the past—to no effect whatsoever—to want to go through that humiliating experience again, to put her pride on the line for him to trample on.

'No,' he said implacably. 'At least, not the one you outline. You surprise me, Cassandra,' he added, as if he questioned her sanity. 'When we married I found work for your brother in the Jerez accounts office because, according to him, he didn't want to cut the apron strings and go back to England without you and he didn't want to follow in your father's footsteps and study medicine. In fact he almost shed tears when I reminded him that that was what his father had wanted.'

'He was barely twenty-one and he didn't know what he wanted to do with his life. He'd not long lost his father, had had to face the fact that the family home had to be sold to pay Dad's debts—and, unlike you, he hadn't come into this world cushioned by money and holding the entrenched belief that he was superior to everyone else on the planet!'

He ignored her protective outburst as if the heated words had never been said, just as he had ignored every opinion, every need of hers, in the past. 'I gave Roy a job with a living wage, then paid the rent on an apartment because after a while he complained that he wanted to be independent of the family household in Jerez. He repaid me by going in to the office late and leaving early—when he bothered to go at all—and finally betrayed me and my family by embezzling a not insubstantial amount of money.' He lifted his shoulders in a dismissive shrug, as if the conversation was beginning to bore him. 'Having you rescue him from the consequences of his crime and repay the money he stole would not build his character, I think.'

Cassie winced. She hated to admit it, but in a way he was right. But she knew her brother far better than Roman did, and a spell in prison wouldn't help Roy achieve responsible adulthood.

She put her fingers to her temples. The pain was getting worse. She'd made this journey, come face to face with Roman again, had the humiliation of seeing her offer brushed aside as if it had been made by a fool, and accomplished precisely nothing. She felt as if she'd been chewed up and spat out, and it wasn't a pleasant sensation. She pushed herself to her feet.

'If that's your final word, I'll leave, but I'd like to see Roy before I go,' she said thickly. 'I'll wait here until he finishes work.' Surely he couldn't be heartless enough to deny her that? She had to see her twin, let him know she'd done her best. Advise him to take his punishment like a man and tell him to come back to England, to her, when he was free, and she'd do everything she could to help him to make a fresh start.

'And here was I, beginning to think you'd developed a backbone,' he said lightly. 'I think you give up too easily.'

Perspiration was slicking her skin and she folded her arms jerkily across her chest as she tried to contain the feeling that she was about to have hysterics. 'And I think you don't know what you're talking about,' she said, hanging on to what little poise she had left. 'You won't listen to what I have to say so what am I supposed to do? Sit in my chair like a good little girl until I grow roots?'

'I listened,' Roman remarked with an indolence that made her hackles rise.

She felt her face go red. 'Maybe. But you still refused to consider what I said!'

'I wasn't aware that it was mandatory.' One broad shoulder lifted in a very slight shrug.

He was impossible! Swallowing fury, she hitched the strap of her bag over her shoulder. She was leaving! But easier said than done, because a graceful long-legged stride, one hand on her arm, stopped her.

She didn't want him touching her. The heat of his hand through the fine fabric of her sleeve brought back memories she had no desire to acknowledge. Her tongue, though, was welded to the roof of her mouth and, before she could unstick it, he said at a smooth tangent, 'You've gained weight. For most of our two years together you reminded me of a stick. Sometimes I used to worry about you.'

What a lie! Concern for her happiness and well-being had been so low on his list of priorities it had fallen off the bottom of the paper!

'Liar!' she accused scornfully. 'The only people who worried about my weight loss were your mother and aunts. And that, according to the precious Delfina, was because they thought I was anorexic and possibly infertile. She even told me that having your child was the only way they would ever accept me.' Seized by a wild, uncontrollable anger, she surged on, 'I should have told them that I lost weight because I was desperately unhappy. That I couldn't conceive because you never came near me!'

The words blistered her mouth but she didn't regret them. It was time Roman faced the truth.

'I thought you didn't want me to?' The sensual line of his mouth tightened. 'You rejected me, or don't you remember?'

It was framed as a question but he'd wait until hell froze over before he got an answer. She'd die before she admitted how much she'd regretted pushing him away, turning from him, lacking the courage to tell him how she felt; how later she'd ached for his touch; how his indifference, his long absences had hurt her.

She thinned her mouth as, probably in retaliation for her stubborn silence, glittering charcoal eyes veiled by thick black lashes made a lazy inventory of the curves she privately thought had grown a little too lush just lately. Her body burned hotly where his eyes touched and she tried to squirm away, aware that her breath was thick in her throat. His unanswered question and the explicitly intimate way he was looking at her was beginning to fill her with embarrassment and confusion.

What did he know about how she had felt? The sense of inadequacy, the beginnings of the shame that had grown right throughout their marriage because he had obviously decided she was frigid, not worth the trouble of going to her room at night.

His fingers tightened on her arm, his other hand resting lightly on her waist, just above the feminine roundness of her hips; his voice was sultry and wicked as he asked, 'I wonder if a year apart has made any difference? Perhaps we should try to find out. Would you still reject me if I came to you in the night?'

'Don't!' It was wrenched from her. She went rigid. She had taught herself not to cry; she wasn't going to forget those harsh lessons and disgrace herself now.

Once—it seemed like a lifetime ago now—she had thought she loved him, had worshipped him, believed him to be the most perfect being ever to draw breath.

Now she knew better. He couldn't get to her on any level if she didn't let him. She threw back her head and challenged him, 'If you think I'm going to oblige you, lie down on the floorboards while you satisfy your sexual curiosity, then you can think again!'

She slapped his hands away, one after the other, and headed for the door, her lips clamped together to stop herself screaming with all the remembered pain, and he drawled behind her, 'I had something rather more civilised in mind, *mi esposa*. Share my bed for the next three months and satisfy my...sexual curiosity, and I won't bring charges against your brother.'

CHAPTER TWO

'You need time to think about it?' Roman asked as the brittle silence stretched until it was painful. The soft, almost scornful strand of amusement in his voice finally snapped her out of her state of numbing shock.

'You can't be serious!' The thin, wavery bleat of her own voice secretly appalled her. She hadn't meant to sound so utterly withering. Cassie swallowed convulsively and tried again, tried to do better. 'You must be desperate if you have to resort to blackmail to get a woman to share your bed!'

This time the contempt she felt must have echoed in her tone because she saw his eyes narrow, his jawline harden. He was a passionate man; she knew that—passionate about his work, the land he loved, the family name, his women. Never about *her*, though, and they both knew it. Her taunt would have damaged his inbred, fierce Spanish pride.

'Not blackmail—a condition,' he corrected harshly. 'Non-negotiable. You are free to take my offer, or leave it.'

'My body's not a commodity to be bartered,' she stated, suddenly feeling shivery, as if her flesh had been plunged into a deep freeze. What he was suggesting was completely out of the question.

But he obviously wasn't seeing it that way because his voice roughened. 'It was before, if I remember correctly. Your body in my bed in exchange for my ring on your finger, a life of luxury, payment of your father's debts—and let's not forget that nice soft option for your brother, which we now know he abused. And again, with you, I got the rough end of the bargain and found myself sharing a bed with a block of ice. My bride made me feel like an animal with depraved and intolerable appetites—it was not an experience I wished to repeat.'

So he had left her completely alone. And he hadn't had the sense to understand that she'd been terrified.

Not of him, because she had loved him then, but scared half to death of failing the shatteringly sexy, passionate and experienced man who had swept her off her feet with one smile from those sensually moulded lips, one glance from those sultry, smoky eyes. The man who hadn't seen that his family's displeasure at his choice of wife had already made her feel inferior and totally inadequate.

And she hadn't had the courage to explain all of that to him, to at least try to tell him how she felt. Cassie shook that unwanted thought out of her head and closed her eyes as she dragged in a deep lungful of air; when she opened them he was holding the door open, his powerful body graceful, relaxed.

Showing her out? Bored? Impatient to get rid of

her now he knew she would have nothing to do with his outrageous suggestion?

So why did she feel giddy with relief when he told her, 'I'm not suggesting something immoral. You are my wife.'

'We're separated,' she reminded him, defensively putting her light-headedness down to the trauma of the last few days, the expenditure of courage that had been needed to bring her to face him again.

'Not by my wish,' he stated dismissively. He swung on his heels.

Catching her breath, she followed him along the stone-flagged passageway that connected the old farmhouse to the newer, more comfortable addition that had been built in his father's lifetime. Surely there was room for negotiation? Surely she could make him see that his cruel suggestion simply wasn't practical, then ask him to reconsider her original offer?

'Roman!' If there was a desperate edge to her voice, she couldn't help it. Her brother's future depended on her ability to make her estranged husband change his mind. 'Even if I wanted to come back to you—' which she most definitely did not '—I couldn't. I have a living to earn, a job to go back to. I told Cindy I'd only be away for a couple of days. It's one of our busiest times.'

He stopped, turned, his impressive figure framed in the archway that led into the main hall. He lifted wide shoulders dismissively. 'No problem. I'll phone my cousin and explain. She'll understand.'

Of course she would! Cindy idolised Roman, she hadn't been able to believe her ears when Cassie had returned to England with the news that her marriage was over.

The relationship wasn't as close as Roman had stated. Cindy's grandmother had been Doña Elvira's eldest sister. She'd married a Scot and they'd lived in England, producing Cindy's mother. Although the Fernandez family hadn't approved of the alliance with a mere foreigner, Doña Elvira and her surviving sisters had remained in contact.

Cassie and Cindy had been best friends since they'd met at school as five-year-olds, and it had been to her and her warm and loving family that Cassie had turned when her and Roy's father had died from a heart attack.

They couldn't have been more supportive. When the shock news had come that the house Cassie and Roy shared with their widowed father would have to be sold to cover his debts, Cindy's mother had suggested, 'We've been planning a holiday in Spain, visiting relatives on my mother's side. Why don't you and Roy come with us? I know they'll make you welcome when I explain the circumstances. And it would give you and Roy a chance to get your heads round what's happened.'

That was how she'd met Roman; that was when the short and, with hindsight, strangely distant courtship had begun. And the rest, she thought tiredly, was history. A history she wished had never been written.

'Any other objections?' he enquired flatly. 'Or is

the resumption of our marriage for three short months too high a price to pay?'

Much, much too high! Roy had done wrong and the only way Roman would allow him to avoid punishment was to punish her in her brother's stead. Their wedding night had been a total fiasco. Although they had consummated the marriage, her fear of disappointing him had made her about as responsive as a lump of rock, thereby ensuring that the experience was one she didn't want to repeat. The fear of further failure had made her push him away when he'd tried to take her in his arms on the following nights after that. So why would he want to force her to share his bed now—unless it was to dole out punishment?

Oh, her objections were legion! Moistening her dry lips with the tip of her tongue, she framed the words of the only one that wasn't personally insulting to him—which meant it was the tritest. 'I came prepared for an overnight stay in Jerez before getting a flight back to England. How can I stay when I haven't got much more than the clothes I'm wearing now?'

His smile was thin and it didn't reach his eyes. 'I think we might be able to find a store that stocks female clothing somewhere in Spain, don't you? And, Cassandra—' his eyes narrowed to slits of smoke-hazed jet '—I'm not prepared to discuss this further. You take my offer, or you leave it. Sleep on it and give me your decision in the morning.' He turned again, lobbing over his shoulder, 'I'll get someone to show you to a room you can use for tonight. We eat at nine, as you may remember, and afterwards you and Roy can have some time together to discuss your futures.'

Dispiritedly, she watched as he strode across the polished terracotta tiles of the airy, square hallway. She had honestly believed she was mature enough now to stand her ground against that overweening authoritarianism of his—that she would never again allow him to tell her what to do, where to go.

Yet she had to admit, after one of the maids—new since her own departure, just over a year ago—had shown her to a bedroom overlooking the courtyard at the back of the house, that her interview with Roman had sapped her of the energy she would have needed to arrange for a taxi to pick her up here and drive her back to Jerez, where she would have had to find overnight accommodation.

Also, this way she was guaranteed some time with her twin. She could sit through dinner with Doña Elvira and the dreadful aunts for the sake of the opportunity to speak to Roy alone afterwards. If she insisted on leaving now, Roman would make sure she didn't get so much as a glimpse of her brother.

She needed to apologise in person for having failed him. Break the news that Roman would be bringing charges against him. It made her sick just to think of it. She'd been looking out for him ever since their mother had died a few days before their eighth birthday, but the price Roman was demanding was way too high. She had worked hard to turn her life around. How could anyone expect her to put herself back in the prison she'd escaped from a year ago?

Her pale face set, she gave the room she'd been shown to a cursory glance. It was very similar to the one she'd used when she'd spent the greater part of her two years of marriage here. Roman had simply dumped her, leaving her with his mother and the aunts while he'd been away doing his own thing. Business in Jerez and Cadiz, with plenty of fringe benefits in the form of fancy restaurants, fancy females, climbing in the Himalayas, skiing at Klosters—whatever turned him on.

Shrugging, consigning her memories back into the past, she unpacked her overnight bag. Cotton nightdress, a change of underwear, make-up and toiletries. Her heart hovering somewhere beneath the floorboards, she went to the adjoining bathroom for a much-needed shower and wished she and her twin had never heard of Roman Fernandez.

Candles—dozens of them—set in shallow crystal bowls imparted a warm, flickering glow to the old silver of the elaborate place settings. Dinner at Las Colinas Verdes was always a formal affair and tonight all the stops had been pulled out because there were two guests.

Herself the unwanted one. And Delfina The Desirable, who had been flavour of the month amongst Roman's female relatives for as long as Cassie had known them.

Roman was seated at the head of the long table with the Spanish woman on his left. Delfina was as exquisite as Cassie recalled, her dark hair cut in a fashionable jaw-length bob, her slender figure clothed in ruby satin, leaving the delicate sweep of her shoulders and arms bare.

'You are looking well, Cassandra. Better than I have seen you. You are obviously happier in your own country.' Doña Elvira, remote and dignified in black silk, was seated at the foot of the table, to Cassie's right. Her remark was made in her perfect English and carried the customary barb.

'Thank you.' Cassie inclined her head coolly. She could have answered that she would have been ecstatically happy in Spain if her husband had loved her, if his family had accepted her. But what was the point raking over a past that was dead and buried as far as she was concerned? She would not let this ordeal undermine her hard-won poise. She wouldn't let any one of them intimidate her now.

Tía Agueda and Tía Carmela, Roman's aunts, were seated opposite, their small dark eyes constantly flicking between Cassie and Delfina. Delfina was speaking in animated Spanish to Roman who, naturally, took pride of place at the head of the gleaming mahogany table. Her hand was continually moving to touch the back of his, or to linger on the white fabric of his sleeve, as if to emphasis a point she was making, her dark eyes flicking and flirting beneath the lustrous sweep of her lashes.

During her time in Spain Cassie had picked up

enough of the language to get by, but the other
woman's voice was pitched too low, too soft and
intimate to allow her to hear what was being said.

She fingered the stem of her wine glass and, as if
noting the unconsciously nervous gesture, Doña
Elvira said, 'It is an uncomfortable time for all of
us.'

And wasn't that the truth? Cassie speared a sliver
of tender pork fillet. Her twin was conspicuous by
his absence. House arrest, he'd told her. He probably
had to eat in the kitchen with the servants. She laid
down her fork, the food unwanted.

'I'll be returning to England tomorrow,' she stated,
squashing the wicked impulse to tell her mother-in-
law of her son's attempt to blackmail her into resum-
ing their marriage. Only for three short months—but,
even so, Doña Elvira and the aunts would hate that.
They were probably already counting down to when
Roman could be free of his unsuitable, hopeless wife
and they could begin pressing him to marry someone
of his own nationality, someone with breeding and
lots of lovely old money!

Something clicked inside her brain. Of course! She
could see it all now. Roy's fall from grace had given
Roman the leverage he needed. It wasn't just sexual
curiosity about her, as he'd so insultingly claimed—
his family must be nagging him again to produce an
heir, and this time he could put them off if it appeared that he was having another stab at making his
marriage work!

Sharply, her mind skidded back to the afternoon

Roman had proposed to her. The older family members had been taking a siesta; Roy and Guy—Cindy's older brother—had taken a couple of horses out onto the *campos* while Cindy and her mother were upstairs packing. About to follow suit—the month-long holiday was over and they were leaving for home the next day—she'd been halfway up the handsomely carved staircase when Roman's softly voiced request had stopped her in her tracks.

'Cassie, got a few minutes to spare?'

Her hand had shot out and tightened on the polished banister until her knuckles stood out like white sea-shells as a wave of raw heat flooded her body. She had been sure she was in love with him, helplessly and hopelessly in love, and it had turned her into a gibbering idiot when he was around.

Cindy had said, *'Mucho macho!'*, pretending to swoon. 'He doesn't even notice me but he follows you with his eyes, you lucky pig!'

Trying not to think of the gross stupidity of that remark—why should a man as gorgeous, as self-assured and wildly wealthy as Roman spare a very ordinary woman with no social skills and about as much sex appeal as a carrot a second glance?—she had waited until the gauche heat ebbed from her face before slowly turning.

He had been watching her from the foot of the stairs. Watching. Waiting. Her throat muscles had gone into spasm.

'I want to talk to you.'

'Yes?' Had her expression been intelligent, or just

plain dumb? The latter, she suspected, because the slight shake of his dark, handsome head, the very slight abrasiveness of his voice had suggested impatience.

'Not here. In the courtyard, for privacy. Come down.'

She'd gone; of course she had. If he'd asked her to walk to the North Pole with him she'd have gone without a murmur. And the sun-soaked courtyard had been deserted except for just the two of them, the scent of the rosemary and lavender planted in the centre perfuming the hot air. And his proposal had been the very last thing she'd expected.

'As my mother and aunts never tire of telling me, it's time I married and sired an heir. They've been dangling suitable females under my nose for the past five years and now that I've reached the venerable age of thirty-three they've stepped up their campaign.

'I tell them to hold their meddling tongues, to put the succession of simpering creatures back into the boxes they dug them out of; I tell them that I will marry the woman of my choosing, not theirs. It makes no difference and, quite frankly, Cass, I am tired of it.'

At that point he had taken her hand and her whole body had melted, turning her into an amorphous mass of sensation, blanking out every last one of her brain cells. What else could explain the unseemly haste, the total lack of logical thought that had accompanied her acceptance when he'd increased the pressure of his fingers on hers and murmured, 'I think we could make a successful marriage. You're young for your years. Don't take that as a criticism— you lack the guile and artifice that bores me in other women, and I find that very appealing. I do need an heir, and for that I need to marry. I want a woman I can live with, a woman whose primary concerns aren't the perfection of her appearance, attending parties that take her days to prepare for, or empty-headed gossip.'

His mouth had indented wryly. 'The bargain wouldn't be one-sided. Since the death of your father you're a ship without a rudder; I gather that he had you convent-educated then used emotional blackmail to keep you at home acting as an unpaid house-keeper. Cass, marriage and motherhood would give you the direction you want. And no need to worry about the debts waiting for you at home—naturally, as your husband, I would discharge them. And for me—' his eyes had softened as he'd smiled into hers '—I would be free of the endless carping from my female relatives. In time, there would be our children to take their meddling minds away from me, and I could get on with my life in peace. And, more importantly, I would have a wife I'd chosen for myself. Will you think about it, dear Cassie?'

She hadn't, she thought now, defiantly draining her wine glass. She'd simply accepted him and thought about it later, when it was too late to do anything other than acknowledge the fact that he had married her because she was biddable, undemanding, a creature of no consequence, and someone he could hide in a corner and forget about. Someone to provide him with the heirs the vast Fernandez estates needed.

Only it hadn't worked out like that, had it?

'I see Delfina still visits you,' she remarked coolly to her mother-in-law. Her voice dripped with sarcasm as she added, 'So kind, don't you think, when sophisticated social events, glitzy restaurants and expensive shops are her natural milieu? Or so she always led me to believe.'

Before, she would never have dreamed of saying such a thing. She had almost literally withered away whenever her mother-in-law or the aunts had spoken to her, almost always with some criticism or other—the way she dressed, her apparent inability to conceive or keep her husband at her side, her weight loss.

'She has always been fond of my son.' Doña Elvira dabbed her mouth with her napkin. 'As I said, it has been an uncomfortable time for all of us.'

Was that sympathy in the older woman's eyes? Cassie thought so. She pulled her lower lip between her teeth. Formerly, had she only listened to the words, failing to see the concern for her well-being and happiness that lay behind the apparent criticisms?

She laid down her napkin, made her excuses, and left the room without even glancing at Roman. Sympathy from a most unexpected quarter wasn't worth thinking about. Not now. It was over.

* * *

'Sis!'

As Cassie closed the door to the formal dining room behind her Roy emerged from beneath the stone arch that led to the kitchen quarters. It took her two seconds to reach him. She wanted to shake him but he looked so wretched she hugged him instead.

'I couldn't sit through dinner, not knowing whether you'd persuaded Roman to give me another chance.'

She had meant to tell him that she'd tried and failed, that he was on his own now and had to take the consequences of his dishonesty, but she could feel his wiry body shaking. Her heart lurched. Her eyes filled with tears.

In the past she'd fought all his battles for him. Maybe he would have been a stronger character if she hadn't. Maybe she was to blame for the way he'd messed up his life.

But how could she fail him now, when he needed her most?

'It will be all right,' she told him unsteadily. 'You'll be given another chance. Make the most of it, though, because it will be your last.'

CHAPTER THREE

THE kitchen was in the older, original part of the house; the stone walls were painted white and the huge black range added to the warmth of the early morning. Asunción, who ran the household and catered for the unmarried estate workers with unruffled efficiency, was kneading dough; two of the maids sat at the other end of the central table, chattering over their toasted rolls and coffee.

'Have you seen Señor Fernandez?' Cassie asked as her appearance made the housekeeper stop pummelling and the maids fall silent.

Unless they'd changed their habits during the past twelve months, Doña Elvira and the aunts wouldn't surface until after they'd breakfasted in their rooms at ten. But when he was here Roman was always out on the estate soon after sunrise; she didn't want to miss him and hang around until lunchtime, getting more nervous and downhearted with every passing second. She wanted to get this over with.

'No, not this morning, *señora*.' Asunción planted her floury hands on her wide hips, her small dark eyes sparking with curiosity. 'Señorita Delfina waits for him also.' One of the maids smothered a giggle, earning a quick dark look from the housekeeper. 'If you join her in the courtyard, someone will bring coffee out for you.'

'Thank you, Asunción.' Cassie retreated smartly, her cheeks burning. Las Colinas Verdes was like a small village; everyone knew everyone else's business and the affairs of the family were the subject of eternal gossip and conjecture.

They would all be wondering why the runaway, unsuitable English wife had returned and why *el patrón* had taken his young brother-in-law out of his comfortable office in Jerez and put him to work like a labourer in the fields. Uncomfortably, she wondered what answers they'd come up with.

She had no wish to join Delfina but she really did need that coffee. Her night had been restless, tormented by the knowledge of what she'd let herself in for. She couldn't go back on her promise to Roy, but if Roman wanted her to pretend that they were making a fresh start, and get his relatives off his back, then she had a condition of her own to make, she thought firmly.

Delfina was sitting in the shade of the sprawling fig tree which grew against one of the high stone walls of the courtyard. She was wearing form-fitting stretch jodhpurs and a cream-coloured, heavy silk shirt; the long sleeves were casually rolled up to just beneath her elbows, displaying lightly tanned forearms and a matching pair of thin gold chain bracelets.

She looked every inch the aristocrat, as if she belonged here. Cassandra couldn't understand why Roman was going to such lengths to pretend he wanted another shot at making his marriage to an average-looking nobody like her work, when surely he could see that this beautiful, sophisticated daughter of a wealthy sherry family would make him a perfect wife. Or had he really meant it when he'd said that Delfina's type bored him?

'If you're looking for Roman, you're out of luck,' Delfina snapped. 'We had a date to go riding but he must have left without me.' The lovely, perfectly made-up face was petulant, the scarlet mouth drooping sulkily. 'He always did head for the hills rather than spend time around you, so I guess that's what's happened now.'

'Is that so?' Cassie slid on to the bench seat on the opposite side of the table, in the full glare of the already hot sun, noting that the other woman had barely touched her coffee or her juice. Roman might enjoy the flirtatious attentions of Delfina, and the way she hung around him would boost his already considerable ego. But he certainly wouldn't want to marry her, and not only because her shallowness would bore him.

Delfina had been born to elegance and style, and was accustomed to the high life. She certainly wouldn't allow herself to be isolated here, seeing her husband only when he felt like dropping by for a week or two, producing babies and closely chaperoned by his mother and aunts while he swanned off, free as a bird. She would make a demanding wife, while he had wanted a dutiful, self-effacing one, one

who didn't ask questions or demand a single thing
of him.

Roman Fernandez was far too selfish to completely tie himself down to a woman; he enjoyed the
pleasures of a bachelor-style life far too much. But
at least, Cassie knew, he wouldn't seduce the other
woman. She came from an important family and he
wouldn't compromise her; his Spanish code of honour wouldn't let him. Though why she should see
that as a consolation, Cassie couldn't imagine. She
no longer cared what he did.

'I can't think why you came back after all this
time,' Delfina said pettishly. 'You're wasting your
time if you expect Roman to take you back—because
he won't, you know. How long are you staying, anyway?' she wanted to know. 'It can't be too long if
the only thing you've got with you is the same old
suit you wore to dinner last night,' Delfina added
disparagingly. 'And you really shouldn't sit in the
sun, not with your ginger colouring. You'll get covered in ghastly freckles, just like your brother. And
what's he doing working here? I thought Roman had
given him an easy life back in the office in Jerez.'

'He's learning estate management from the bottom
up,' Roman's dark, velvety voice supplied. He was
standing in the shadow of the pillared arcade that
surrounded the courtyard on three sides. 'And you
never know, if he's not otherwise engaged when
Miguel retires in six years' time, Roy might make
manager.'

Cassie got the message. Roy could make something of himself here on the estate, or go to prison. She shivered, despite the warmth of the sun. At least Roman hadn't confided the true situation to Delfina. She offered up a silent word of thanks for his tact.

'We had a date,' the Spanish woman cooed as Roman stepped out of the shadows. The petulance gone, she was all smiling welcome. She stood up, smoothing her hands over her prettily curved hips. 'I've waited for ages, but at least you're here now— so just this once I've decided to forgive you!'

He wasn't dressed for riding. Wearing narrow fawn-coloured cotton trousers topped by a black shirt in the finest lawn, he looked fantastic, all raw male sexuality—and then some. Cassie knew exactly why Delfina couldn't keep away from him; she could imagine how the Spanish woman's hopes would have soared when she'd learned that his failure of a wife had left him.

Cassie almost felt sorry for her!

'You're going to have to ride alone this morning,' Roman stated abruptly, as if his patience was running out. 'I have urgent business with my wife. But,' he added as a palliative, 'I had Demetrio saddle up for you. The mare's ready and waiting in the stable yard.'

His cool smile seemed to soften what was obviously a blow and pushed what petulant words Delfina might have been about to say back down her throat. Asunción, bearing down on them with a huge tray, did the rest.

As the housekeeper, with a murmured, 'Señor,

Señora,' set out breakfast for two and cleared away the offerings Delfina had barely touched, the Spanish girl swept her eyes dismissively over Cassie, gave Roman a commiserating smile and drawled, 'I'll leave you to your boring business then, *caro.* You can make amends for letting me down when you've finished with it.' Another pointed glance in Cassie's direction and then she was walking away, leaving the sultry perfume that was her trademark behind in the hot summer air.

As Asunción left, Roman took the seat Delfina had vacated and Cassie eyed the crispy rolls, honey, fresh fruit and coffee and felt her throat close up. Alone with him, she felt wound up enough to explode, and he made it a thousand times worse when he reached out a hand and ran the back of his fingers lightly down the side of her face.

'Unlike your unidentical twin, your skin doesn't freckle.' His voice was slow, sexy and smooth, the smoky eyes following the movement of his fingers as they rested briefly on the corner of her mouth. 'And I wouldn't describe your hair as ginger—far more like burnished chestnuts, Cassie.'

After those first few disastrous days of their honeymoon he'd never touched her, except perhaps by accident. He'd certainly never touched her skin deliberately, lingeringly, seductively. So why touch her now? Why was he trying to contradict Delfina's earlier insults? Her huge eyes were bewildered.

She tried to move, to jerk her head away from the gentle stroke of his fingers, the warmth that was setting fire to her skin—but she was mesmerised, trapped beneath the intimacy of his eyes, for all the world as if she were twenty-one years old again. Vulnerable, gullible, innocent and still traumatised by recent happenings.

'Awwwk—' The sound that emerged from her painfully tight throat was more like a croak than the opening for a sensible statement. As if he knew he could sweet-talk her into a state of feeble submission where his threats had failed, one dark brow quirked upwards; a slight smile curved his sensual mouth as he dropped his hand and lifted the coffee pot.

But it wasn't that; it really wasn't. She was beyond all that self-serving charm. It was just that she dreaded having to commit herself, but knew she had to if she were to save her twin.

And now—apart from that condition she was determined to make—the time had come to tell him she agreed to accept his monstrous offer.

She could hardly believe this was happening to her. It had taken courage to walk out on him, and a whole lot of determination to put him and what he had meant to her right out of her mind.

Her throat jerking, she swallowed around the constriction in her throat, stared into the rich, steaming coffee he had placed in front of her and stated as evenly as she could manage, 'If you must use me to divert your family from pestering you to provide an heir then I'll stay with you for the three months you stipulated. But—'

'A diversion? Interesting…' Roman looked almost amused.

'What other reason could you have?' Suddenly, Cassie was wary.

'None.' A glint of wickedness in the dark eyes belied the blunt disclaimer, but she was reassured by his, 'You catch on quickly; well done! You are my wife, you're here, and you suit my purposes—but don't forget, the deal includes you sleeping with me, as a good wife should…'

Cassie swallowed hard and forced an edge into her voice, 'Point taken. You don't have to paint a picture. I'll keep my part of the bargain, but not here.'

'Is that an ultimatum, *mi esposa*?'

'Take it or leave it.' She echoed his former words, trying to blank out the knowledge that he was not a man to be coerced, trying to look as if she wouldn't back down while all the time knowing that she would have to if he didn't agree.

'I wonder what it is about Las Colinas Verdes that you dislike so much?' he queried idly. Cassie shot him a suspicious glance from beneath her lashes. Buttering a roll, spreading it with honey, he gave every appearance of being totally relaxed about the whole surreal situation. 'I seem to recall a previous time when you asked if we might make a home somewhere else.'

She hadn't simply asked, she'd begged—practically pleaded with him on her knees! She hadn't been able to bear being left here, watched over and criticised by his mother and his aunts, enduring Delfina's visits—visits which had always miraculously coincided with Roman's own.

But he had barely listened. But then why should he have when her misery—the feeling of being abandoned, a prisoner—hadn't been important to him? After their disastrous wedding night, it had suited him to have her out of sight and out of mind.

'It isn't the place,' she corrected sharply. 'It's the people.' And if that was insulting to his family, tough! She had grown out of pussy-footing around him, trying to please him, vainly hoping he would start to feel something for her beyond indifference. 'If we were here, they'd be watching like hawks to see if I got pregnant. I've been there, done that. And I don't want a repetition.'

'You could have told them they were wasting their time,' he said coldly. 'That the likelihood of your conceiving my child was non-existent because you couldn't bear me to touch you.'

Cassie swallowed the instinctive, vehement response that the blame for that was just as much his as hers. After all, she'd broached this subject yesterday; the snap of his eyes and the tightening of his jaw line had showed her that her criticism of his family had made him angry.

She took a deliberate sip of coffee, then took a deep breath and made her tone entirely reasonable as she told him, 'I don't want to get into a fight, Roman. Our marriage was a mistake. It didn't work for all sorts of reasons. The past is best forgotten; it's no longer important. What matters right now is deciding how we're going to handle the next three months, and where we'll spend them.'

Another few sips while she weathered the startling frisson that racketed through her body at the mere thought of the coming three months. And, if anything, her prosaic words—meant to pour oil on waters that were beginning to look ominously turbulent—seemed to have worsened the situation, because his black brows were drawn together, his haughty Spanish disdain sharp enough to cut.

'We'll spend them together. That was the bargain.' He got to his feet, the dappled shade reinforcing the mystery of the man. He was a complex character, many-faceted; she had never been able to understand him. 'I will break the news of our reconciliation to my family. Be ready to leave in an hour.'

His mouth pulled back against his teeth, he stared down at her, as if daring her to say another word, then swung round and walked away. He left her wondering at his change of mood.

Set to charm the socks off her to start with—most probably in an attempt to persuade her to fall in with his wishes. Then showing flashes of simmering black temper after she'd agreed to what he wanted: the pretence of a reconciliation!

No, she never had been able to understand him. But it really didn't matter now, did it?

CHAPTER FOUR

BEYOND a few lines of self-consciously banal chit-chat, they had barely spoken. The prickly silence inside the air-conditioned car was beginning to get to Cassie, but it didn't seem to bother Roman and that annoyed her.

Everything had happened so quickly her throbbing head was still going round in ever accelerating circles.

Yesterday they'd driven away from the *finca*, the vast Las Colinas Verdes estate, leaving behind Doña Elvira and the aunts, who had looked as if they didn't know what had hit them, Delfina, who knew very well what had hit her and hated it very much indeed, and a suitably chastened and contrite Roy.

Roy had hurriedly assured her in a last-minute undertone that he would work his socks off on the estate to make up for what he had done, adding gruffly, 'Don't worry about me. I've got my head straightened out. Just concentrate on making a go of your marriage this time, sis. Roman's crazy about you; he's been unbearable to be around since you went away.'

Which only went to show that working under the

hot Spanish sun had sent her twin brother completely loopy.

They'd arrived in Seville in the sweltering afternoon heat and booked into a hotel where, to her knee-sagging relief, she'd been given a room of her own, complete with a four-poster bed and wonderful views of the Giralda. Then, before she'd had time to unpack her meagre belongings, Roman had knocked on the door, insisting on taking her to a surprisingly elegant boutique off the pedestrianised Calle Sierpes.

The sheer, rather stark grace of the dark-haired woman who had approached them had made Cassie sit up and take notice. The discreet decor, the clever lighting, the single garment on display—a simple cream silk suit with a designer label to die for— shrieked serious money.

'I need something practical,' Cassie had muttered at Roman, mentally digging her heels in. One or two cotton skirts, trousers and tops plus comfy sandals— stuff that could be bought cheaply at the market, not wickedly expensive designer gear. She hated the thought of being beholden to him to that extent.

A lazy look into her hot and mutinous face, the slight raising of one sable brow, and Roman had smoothly taken over. But when the pile of garments which had been brought out for his inspection and approval had reached mountainous proportions, Cassie had snapped, 'Enough!'

So here she was, with enough beautiful, expensive clothes to last her a lifetime packed into the boot of the Mercedes, driving away from Seville in the hazy warmth of the following morning, her head throbbing sullenly after another sleepless night, her body tense with the misgivings that were accumulating with remorseless rapidity and her mind buzzing with unanswered questions.

One of which was answered as they headed out of Jerez, making for the coast, through the gently undulating vineyards, miles upon miles of them beneath the vast blue sky.

'You're taking me to Sanlucar?' She could hardly believe it. Was he too insensitive to realise that the beautiful stone house, almost a mini-palace, in the old quarter of the historic port, was the last place she wanted to have to see again?

He spared her a mild sideways glance. 'You didn't want to stay on the estate, the house in Jerez is being redecorated, and I remembered how delighted you were with this area, the house. So, yes, we shall make our home in Sanlucar.'

He was talking as though it would be a permanent arrangement. 'For three months,' she reminded him stiffly, the memories she'd thought she'd successfully buried rising up to the surface of her mind to torment her.

He'd brought her to the house in Sanlucar for their honeymoon. She'd fallen in love with the place on sight and had told him as much. The tall rooms, the time-touched, lovingly tended antiques, the perfumed courtyard where water played in the ancient stone fountain and white doves called from the top of the walls where pale lemon roses arched in graceful profusion.

And it had all gone wrong, every single thing; instead of staying for several weeks, they'd left after three days. She'd been weeping silent tears of shame and hopeless inadequacy as they'd driven away and his gorgeous, beloved face had been stiff with Spanish pride. From that moment on he had virtually ignored her existence.

Had he brought her here to humiliate her? Was that another part of her punishment? Probably. A year ago he would have been incredulous, furious, when he'd received that note telling him she was leaving him. No one—not even a despised, unwanted wife—could turn their back on him and hope to get away with it.

And now she was being punished for it.

The large stone house overlooking the mouth of the Guadalquivir was deserted, the elegant, high-ceilinged rooms silent. Roman said, with no particular inflexion whatsoever, 'The caretaker and his wife are on leave. I thought it best to give them extra time off under the circumstances. So we fend for ourselves for a week or two. In view of your recent independence, I'm sure you won't find that a problem.'

'None at all,' she answered blandly. 'Housekeeping will help pass the time.' Not for the world would she let him see that their isolation worried her, that the thought of sharing his bed—as he had stipulated—horrified her, made her feel almost as if she were prostituting herself.

Her amber eyes were expressionless as they locked with his. He had married a naïve, vulnerable dreamer. Three years on she had her feet firmly on the ground, an adult woman toughened by harsh experience. It was something he was going to have to learn.

She said stiffly, 'I'll leave you to dispose of the luggage.' Heaps of it littered the shady hall. 'Is there a phone still in the small salon? I need to call Cindy.'

'That's already been taken care of.' He was watching her narrowly. 'She was delighted to hear we would be living as man and wife again,' he told her, a thread of cruelty hardening his voice. 'You have nothing to say to her that has not already been said.'

'I think,' she said calmly, ignoring the flutter of nerves that notched her heartbeats up a gear, 'that I'm the best judge of that.' She turned her back on him and began to walk away. Never again would he tell her what to do and expect her to submit in the old mindless fashion. She had moved on. She had changed.

But she was actually shaking as she dialled her friend's number, fine tremors that ruffled the surface of her skin and sent mini-icebergs bobbing through her veins. Standing up to Roman instead of taking the much easier option and acting like a doormat was strangely exhilarating. She felt as if she were stepping blindfold into unknown, scary territory.

'Dolls and Dames, how may I help you?' The

sound of Cindy's bright voice curved Cassie's mouth in a wistful smile. She could hear the chatter of customers in the background, the hypnotic beat of the latest chart-topper, and she wished ferociously that she was back there, in the thick of things, getting on with her own life.

'It's me,' she said. 'I'm sorry about what's happened—Roman said he'd already spoken to you. Look, Cin, about my job and the flat—' Would they still be waiting for her at the end of three months? 'I'll be back, I promise, I—'

'Stop fussing,' Cindy inserted blithely, her voice raised against the background noise. 'And for heaven's sake don't apologise. It's the best news I've heard in a long while. The only person who isn't celebrating because you and Roman have got back together is Guy. He looks like he's won the lottery and lost the ticket! My poor brother hoped to move in on you after you and Roman divorced, so now he's stuck in the mother and father of sulks. But don't you worry yourself about that, or anything, you hear me? Enjoy your second honeymoon—Sanlucar, Roman told me—and come back to clear your personal stuff from the flat when you feel like it. And don't worry about dropping me in the you-know-what because I hired a school-leaver yesterday—seventeen and sassy. She stepped right into your shoes as if they'd been hand-made for her.'

Glumly, Cassie gave up. Obviously, to save face, her estranged husband had intimated that the supposed reconciliation would be of a permanent duration. He had lost her a job she enjoyed and her home. However loudly she might protest that she wouldn't stay in Spain a minute longer than three months, her friend wouldn't believe her.

'I had no idea Guy felt that way,' she said disbelievingly when she was able to get a word in. 'You have to be wrong. We've been friends for ever. Just friends,' she insisted.

'Nope. My big brother started fancying his chances with you on the holiday we all had in Spain—but Roman made his move, and the next we knew you'd promised to marry him. Poor old Guy— back home he started to sow wild oats with a vengeance, but as soon as you came back, saying your marriage was over, he stopped dating and started waiting for your divorce to come through. He didn't think it right to tell you how he felt until you were free.'

'Oh, Lord!' Cassie pressed the knuckles of her free hand against her forehead. 'I promise you, I didn't realise.' Just one more thing to worry about. Guy was almost like another brother; she hated to think she had caused him misery, albeit unknowingly.

When she came off the phone she tried to put the unsettling conversation out of her mind. She had more pressing matters to deal with. Roman had disappeared, and so had the luggage.

Suddenly, all those beautiful new clothes seemed utterly desirable. Refusing to make use of them because he had bought them seemed childish. Cutting her nose off to spite her face. The suit she'd travelled to Spain in felt as if it had been on her back for a year!

She mounted the magnificent staircase, the banister supports intricately carved with clusters of grapes and exotic birds, trying to ignore the fluttery sensations in the pit of her stomach. 'Bedroom' and 'Roman' were not words she was happy to couple together.

With diminishing hope, she poked her head into one bedroom after another. No sign of her things. As she approached the master suite, the scene of their honeymoon disasters, her heart fluttered wildly. Taking a deep breath to steady it, she opened the elaborately carved door.

Nothing about the beautiful room had been changed. Tall windows overlooked the gardens and the rolling hills beyond the coastal plain. Sumptuous brocade in soft shades of rose and silver covered the walls and the graceful chairs which flanked a low antique table that was perfect for intimate breakfasts for two.

She refused to look at the splendour of the four-poster bed.

The classy carrier bags and her overnight case were piled in the centre of the floor and Roman was hanging his gear in the cavernous wardrobe. He had no intention of letting her wriggle out of her side of the bargain or even to give her a night or two of breathing space!

Well, the room hadn't changed, and he surely hadn't. But she had. She was no longer an inarticulate mouse, unable to express her feelings. She said to the back of his head, 'I see you don't intend to offer me the privacy of my own room. In at the deep end, is it? Hardly a subtle approach.'

The wide shoulders stiffened beneath the crisp white cotton. He turned slowly, his darkly glittering eyes meeting hers and holding.

'Subtlety didn't get me anywhere on our honeymoon here. Or perhaps you've forgotten how you gritted your teeth and endured my lovemaking? Do you know how that made me feel?' he demanded, a dull flush of angry colour staining his craggy cheekbones. 'Little better than an animal, taking my own pleasure and giving none! Cassie—' his tone altered, softening just a little '—I told myself to make allowances for your sheltered upbringing, your total lack of experience. After all, that was part of the attraction I felt for you. But after that first time you wouldn't let me near you. So I left you alone—as you wanted. There's a limit to how many blows to his pride a man can take.'

Her eyes dropped guiltily. She had never looked at it quite like that before. Instinctively, she'd known that what she'd secretly feared had become fact. She'd been a huge disappointment to him on their wedding night, fear of failing him making her freeze, unable to relax or respond.

And that same fear had made her instinctively reject him whenever he tried to touch her again.

If only he'd said one word of love, things might

have been so very different... But then, for all his
faults, Roman wasn't a liar...

'I suggest we drop the subject,' he said flatly.
'Why don't you unpack while I find something for
lunch?'

He walked out, closing the door behind him and,
for no reason that she could think of, she felt totally
bereft.

An hour later she descended the stairs. A shower in
the luxurious green marble *en suite* had worked won-
ders, as had the liberal application of fragrant body
oil.

And the choice of what to wear from the huge
selection of shockingly expensive clothing Roman
had insisted she have had been difficult. Everything
was so lovely.

In the end she'd settled for white lace briefs, soft,
silky wide-legged trousers in a gorgeous tawny colour and a matching halter-neck top that left her arms
and most of her back bare and negated the need to
wear a bra.

She'd left her hair loose and it was beginning to
dry in soft curling tendrils. After adding the barest
touch of lipstick and mascara, she felt ready to go
downstairs. She wasn't going to think about the coming night and get herself all tense and apprehensive
because she might, just might, be able to wriggle out
of it.

She paused for a moment on the cool tiles of the
hall, then followed the sound of cutlery. Roman was

drawing the cork from a bottle of white Rioja and the kitchen table held a huge tray crammed with plates, cutlery, glasses and salads.

The arrogant Roman Fernandez, master of the vast Colinas Verdes estates, working in a kitchen? Unheard of!

'You have been busy,' she drawled from the doorway, amusement in her voice. For some reason, seeing him in an unprecedented domestic role made her feel warm inside.

He glanced up, smoky eyes veiled by twin fans of thick dark lashes. 'I have impressed myself,' he confessed in his lightly accented, sexy voice, his sudden white grin disarming her.

He straightened, placing the opened bottle that was already sporting a haze of condensation on the over-burdened tray, the straight black bar of one eyebrow rising in silent appraisal.

Resting one narrow-boned hip on the side of the table, he let his eyes travel with slow deliberation from the toes of her sandalled feet to eventually lock with hers.

'I was right to insist on that outfit.' His voice was low, sultry. 'You would have thrown it back in that poor woman's face, along with everything else I chose for you. It becomes you. You have beautiful breasts. You were right not to constrict them in a bra.'

His openly sexual appraisal had made her breath catch in her throat. She felt her nipples peak as a slow ache of desire flared deep inside her. Heavens, the man was dynamite! A look, a word, could bring any woman to her knees! No wonder she had felt inadequate, way out of his league.

His narrowed charcoal eyes still held hers as a rapid pulse of embarrassed colour covered her face. 'A mere observation,' he said lightly. His mouth wasn't smiling but his eyes were dancing. 'Shall we eat? Outside?'

He lifted the heavy tray and strode out through the open door. Cassie dragged in a shuddery breath and followed.

In the past she'd only had to look at him to go dizzy with wanting him. Wanting him so badly yet unable to deliver.

If he had his way, the whole humiliating farce was due to begin all over again—unless she could convince him that it wasn't necessary.

By the time she caught up with him he was unloading the contents of the tray on to a teak table in the courtyard. Shaded by a massive almond tree, flanked by ancient stone urns filled with perfumed lilies and carnations, it was the ideal site for a relaxed meal, the prelude to a second honeymoon.

Suddenly, her legs felt hollow. She sat down quickly. It was so hot, even in the green shade that made his skin seem darker, his eyes enigmatic. The combination of the still, heavily perfumed air and nervous tension was making her dizzy.

'You have to be hungry,' he allowed, piling a plate with thin slices of the ham that was a speciality of the region, plump olives and crisp salad. 'Since you

refused to eat breakfast back at the hotel. Tell me—'
his eyes skimmed her wilting body as he poured the
wine '—do I ruin your appetite, Cassie *mia*?
Whenever I was at the *finca* I saw you pick at your
food, yet you've gained weight during this last year.
A very becoming amount of weight.'

Cassie reached for a crusty roll, broke it and driz-
zled olive oil over the two halves. She took a deliberate bite and speared a succulent morsel of ham with
her fork.

'You intimidated me,' she told him honestly. If
nothing else, a year away from him had given her
back the ability to give an opinion, vocalise her
thoughts. 'I was dumped in that isolated farmhouse
with nothing to do but endure the disapproval of your
female relatives. When you did put in an appearance,
you barely seemed to see me—'

'Oh, I saw you,' he slid in, his mouth compressing.
'Whenever I was foolish enough to try to get near
you I saw a pair of frightened eyes, I saw panic. *Por
Dios!* Is it any wonder I stopped trying?'

'That was just sex,' she shot back. 'You wanted
an heir. That was the only use you had for me!' Her
fingers tightened convulsively on the misty surface
of her wine glass. 'When it was obvious that it wasn't
going to happen, you washed your hands of me—
you couldn't even be bothered to ask why!' she told
him stormily. 'What *I* wanted was never important,
was it? When I asked—*begged* you to let us make a
home away from the *finca*—'

'You were hysterical,' he reminded coldly. 'In those days I needed to be away often—'

'You could have taken me with you,' Cassie snapped back, wishing the subject didn't still have the power to make her so angry. The past was dead, so why couldn't she bury it? She drained her glass in one long swallow, hoping the chilled wine would cool her temper.

And when he dismissed, 'My mother was worried about you; the aunts, too, decided you needed guidance, looking after,' she could have hurled the empty glass straight at his head.

As if he read the intention in her eyes he calmly refilled the prospective missile, then put his forearms on the table, leaning towards her.

The shock of soft dark hair that fell over his forehead and his sudden, disarming smile made him look younger than his thirty-six years. And his voice was husky as he told her, '*Querida*, we are not here to quarrel. You have your wish. We are away from the *finca* and my relatives. Now we can see if your attitude in the bedroom has changed as radically as your figure and your ability to answer me back.'

He reached out and touched her hand and the whole of her body caught fire as he said, 'I am looking forward to finding out, *mi esposa*.'

CHAPTER FIVE

THE fluid music of the fountain as the water splashed into the shallow stone basin seemed unnaturally loud in the silence that lay over the courtyard. The way he was still looking at her, the things he had said, released a flood of shattering sensation inside her, making her flesh quiver, her blood pound hotly through her veins. It took her breath away.

Responding to the way he looked, the sound of his voice, his vital masculinity, had never been a problem. Nothing had changed in that respect. But she couldn't deliver, couldn't hope to please and enthrall a man of his sophistication and experience.

Could she?

Feeling as if her bones were about to disintegrate, she gripped the stem of her wine glass and said thickly, 'It needn't happen—the bed thing,' and felt her face go red beneath those steady, watchful eyes.

'I see.' Long fingers lazily plucked a grape from the terracotta platter. She heard the wine-dark fruit crunch between his strong white teeth. 'And how do you work that out?'

At least he wasn't forcefully reminding her of the bargain they'd made, she thought, as she thankfully released the breath she'd been holding. He wasn't getting all macho and Spanish and breathing fire and brimstone from those aristocratically sculpted nostrils! In fact, he looked completely relaxed, one arm hooked across the back of his chair, the other reaching towards the grapes.

Roman in a reasonable, listening mood was pretty bewildering—it made her feel as if she were on another planet, but she wasn't going to knock it!

Hoping it was going to last, she said levelly, 'Tell me if I'm wrong, but this supposed reconciliation of ours is being staged to get your family and Delfina off your case, isn't it?'

No response. He crunched another grape and refilled the wine glass she hadn't noticed emptying.

Despite her best intentions, her voice rose a level. 'When you marry again it won't be to that type of spoiled, demanding socialite. Unless you've altered your mind radically, it will be to a quiet breeding machine, content to stay home while you go out to play.'

Cassie huffed in an infuriated breath. He could at least show some interest in what she'd been saying and agree with her, because she knew she was right. 'Why don't you say something? Anything! Or are we having a one-sided conversation here?'

His slow smile was indulgent, his eyes lazy. 'You have an opinion, Cassandra; I am merely doing you the courtesy of listening to it. So far you've not said anything that invited comment.' His brows lifted just slightly. 'I'm patiently waiting to hear what you have to say about the—what did you call it?—the Bed Thing.'

Patronising horror! But losing her temper wouldn't help. 'Exactly,' she said grittily. 'Just putting the picture straight. So sorry to bore you. If you can't be up-front about it and tell Delfina and your family to get lost instead of insisting on this subterfuge to get you out of a corner—'

Now she was being sarcastic. She really couldn't afford to ruffle his feathers, so she deliberately relaxed her shoulders and sugared her tone a little. 'What I'm trying to say is, I've agreed to live with you for three months. To the interested parties back at the *finca*, it will appear that we're making our marriage work. That's enough. They won't have posted spies here, or put hidden cameras in all the rooms. There's absolutely no need for us to actually sleep together.'

There, she'd said it. Holding her breath, feeling the prickle of perspiration gather on her forehead, she waited for his reaction. Surely he would recognise that her being here with him was enough to get Darling Delfina and his matchmaking relatives off his back? Surely he could have no wish to repeat the frustrating and humiliating experiences of three years ago?

Smoky eyes regarded her narrowly. He stretched his endless legs further under the table and clasped his hands behind his head. In the green shade of the almond tree his expression was shadowed, unreadable.

'Are you on the pill, Cass?'

She widened her eyes at him. With a handful of words he'd pushed her thoughts right out of gear. What had her being on the pill got to do with anything?

'Are you?'

'Yes,' she grudged, and felt her face go hot.

'Ah. I see.' His tone might be smooth, but something dark and dangerous flashed in his eyes as he shifted his position, leaning slightly forwards. 'Who's the lucky man? My cousin Guy? He ogled you when he thought no one was looking, when you visited that first time. You certainly headed in his direction when you left me.'

'Don't be ridiculous!' She moved uncomfortably in her seat. Poor Guy. She'd had no idea he'd thought of her in that way. On that fatal visit she'd had eyes for no one but Roman.

'Who, then?'

He looked unpredictable, dangerous. His pose might be studiedly relaxed but she knew better. He was like a coiled spring. Touch him and he'd snap every which way.

Despite being separated for a year, they were still man and wife. If he thought she'd been making love with someone else after rejecting him, the knife-thrust to his monumental Spanish pride would produce an explosion of awesome proportions.

'No one. My GP recommended I go on the pill to regulate my monthly cycle. It had gone haywire. No other reason. Unlike you, I don't look on sex as being

the be-all and end-all of everything,' she said stilt-
edly.

'Of that, *mi esposa*, I am fully aware.' His mouth
curled wryly as he swung down his arms and pushed
back his chair. 'So I choose to believe you. I had to
ask, you understand. One of us has to use protection.'

So he wasn't prepared to listen to reason!

Her heart leapt and fluttered like a frightened bird.
But he wasn't to know that. She wouldn't give him
the satisfaction of seeing her in a panic.

'Protection? Here was I, thinking that the only reason you married me was to get an heir!' Her voice
was commendably cool, she'd even managed a slight
underlying note of amusement. And knew she'd hit
a nerve when his face tightened.

'I do want an heir. But not one given grudgingly.'

Grudgingly? What did he know about it? What did
he know about the lonely heart that had wished
things could have been different, wished he could
have understood her fears, the way she'd hated and
despised herself for her failings?

She would have loved to have had his child, to
have made a real and loving home with him, away
from his critical relatives.

She stood up quickly; the way he was looming
over her was making her jittery. If he weren't so
bone-shakingly gorgeous she could handle him better. Forget that once she had loved him.

And now they were too close.

Cassie took a quick step back, trying not to think
that when he made her keep her side of their fiendish

bargain they would be a whole lot closer. No point in getting in a state before she had to!

'So—' One large, finely made hand gestured vaguely at the table. 'We clear away? Wash the dishes? Then, maybe, siesta?'

His abrupt change of mood, that slow sexy smile, took her breath away all over again. But she recovered it, recovered herself, turned away and told him, '*You* dismissed the staff. *You* do the dishes. And sex in the afternoon wasn't part of the bargain, as I remember.'

She walked away.

As she stepped beneath the rose-covered arch in the stone wall that separated the courtyard from the extensive gardens her skin prickled, the fine hairs standing on end. It felt as if an army of ants wearing red-hot spiky boots were marching all over her body. Knowing him, he would command her to come right back—and if she refused he'd make her.

But he didn't. Only the sleepy sound of the doves, the faint rustle of a breeze in the gently swaying tops of the eucalyptus trees disturbed the peace of the slow Spanish afternoon. She expelled a shaky breath.

Reprieve.

But not for long. Only until tonight.

And did she mind? Really mind?

The sudden, unwelcome question had her rooted to the spot, her feet seemingly glued to the narrow, paved path. Something sharp and fierce twisted deep inside her, making her squeeze her eyelids together. Her lungs expanded as she dragged air into them, inhaling the scents of the billowing borders, heady lilies, hot spicy geraniums, sweet oleander...

She forced her eyes open. What kind of stupid question was that? Of course she minded! She hated the thought of being used to satisfy his warped curiosity, of being punished for what her twin had done!

What sane woman would want to be forced to share Roman's bed? Loads, she answered herself honestly. And it wouldn't be a question of forcing.

Deeply uncomfortable with the way her thoughts were shaping, she marched on, covering all the winding paths that curved around the massive flowerbeds and passing the airless summer house covered with deep red roses. She finally came to a halt at the barrier of wooden poles that overhung the deep and shady ravine.

Steep sides and tall trees offered shade, and far below she could hear the stream from the hills fall over rocks and chatter its way between moss-covered boulders. It was tempting. Up here, at this time of day and at this time of year, the Andalusian sun was merciless.

She felt as if she were melting, her clothes sticking to her overheated body, an ache building up at the back of her eyes. But the only way down was a steep staircase of stone and her legs felt so wobbly she didn't think she'd be able to make it.

Roman, she thought crossly, was probably lolling in the salon, an electric fan cooling the air, a glass of something long and cold to hand. While she—

'You punish yourself.' His voice was slow and soft, the hands he placed on her shoulders gut-wrenchingly gentle.

She hadn't heard him walk up to her, but the sound of his voice in the sleepy silence of the garden, the touch of his hands, hadn't startled her. Almost as if she had known he would come and she'd been wait-ing.

The tips of his fingers moved over her burning skin and she thought: No, *you* punish me. You make me face the things about myself I don't like—the fear, and the cowardice that stopped me doing any-thing about that fear. I should have told you I was afraid, and made you listen. I wasn't brave enough.

'Too much sun, your skin burns.' He lifted the heavy swathe of hair away from the back of her neck and her breath snagged as his lips touched her nape. 'You taste of salt.' His voice purred. 'And woman.'

Her head was beginning to swim, and it wasn't just the effects of the hot afternoon sun. She wanted to move away, to reinforce the distance that had been growing between them ever since their wedding night, but couldn't make her legs function.

Instead she said shakily, 'I was thinking of climb-ing down there, into the shade,' and sagged weakly back against him as his hands slid down her naked arms, cupping her elbows.

A year ago, if he'd come to her, touched her like this, she would have leapt away like a startled rabbit, terrified to let things go further and allow him to rediscover just how frigid she was.

Now, she was incapable of any movement at all; her body wanted to stay exactly where it was, close to him, and her brain had gone AWOL.

'I've got a better idea.' His hands slid around her body, resting on her midriff. The light pressure of his fingertips sent a shock of feverish tension zinging through her. She could feel the hard jut of his pelvis against the lower part of her back and felt faint at the contact, desperately willing his hands to move higher to cup her breasts, to discover for himself the evidence of erect nipples that strained against the insubstantial barrier of silk.

She wanted to cry out, to beg him to touch her, and almost did, but was achingly glad she hadn't when he said lightly, 'We go back to the house and you can shower and rest. Alone. I won't bother you—if that's why you're staying out here and inviting sunstroke. Later, we'll go out for supper. I can't face doing any more dishes!'

He moved away, walking back towards the house, his stride loose and graceful, and Cassie followed, her face flaming.

He hadn't noticed how her body had become so supple and willing, so eager for his touch, how her breath had shortened. But then, why should he? In his limited experience of her, she had never responded. He wouldn't expect anything to have changed.

Which begged the question of why he had stipulated that they share a bed at all.

To punish her.

Which meant he was cruel, had an unfeeling heart and thought of her as nothing more than an experiment. With the side-effect of getting Delfina and his family off his back.

Well, for Roy's sake she could get through the next three months. Roman expected a wooden woman in his bed and that was what he'd get. The aching desire she'd felt just a few moments ago was nothing to worry about.

She'd wanted Roman to make love to her on their wedding night, but when it had come right down to it she'd turned into a block of ice. The same thing would happen again. He'd soon tire of the silly game and remove himself to another room.

And that would be the end of it.

CHAPTER SIX

'You are safe to walk home?' Roman's voice was threaded with dry amusement and Cassie's amber eyes answered his relaxed mood, gleaming up at him.

Moonlight suited him; he looked really spectacular. But then, when did he not?

'I may have had one glass of Rioja too many—'

'Don't forget the Manzanilla—'

'I'm not.' She wrinkled her nose at him. 'Besides, I ate like a horse—those *langostinos* were to die for, and that sauce!' She kissed her fingers in the air and swallowed a husky giggle. 'Besides, what option do I have? Unless you're offering to carry me?'

For answer he gave her a long assessing look, sweeping from head to toe. Cassie felt the sexual awareness that had been hovering between them all evening crank up another notch or two. Or two hundred. The breeze was moulding the fine cotton of the understatedly elegant shift dress she was wearing tightly to her body and his eyes lingered like a lover's touch on each and every lush curve.

She shivered deliciously, the punch of desire inside her making her legs go weak, and he told her, 'It wouldn't be a problem, but I think the walk would sober you up.'

'I'm not drunk!'

'Tipsy, then?' His gorgeous mouth was straight now, unsmiling, making her want to reach up and touch his lips with hers, to feel them soften, remind him of the promise this night held. For both of them.

'Only a little.' She did her best to sound haughty and dismally failed. And didn't really mind. She was beyond being annoyed with him, having to be forever on the defensive. The evening spent in the little restaurant in the Barrio Alto, the oldest part of the port, had been wonderful from start to finish, and if she'd had too much wine it had only been because she'd decided to dull her senses so that the prospect of the coming night might take on less alarming proportions.

Instead, she realised as she took his proffered arm, the alcohol had crept insidiously through her veins, whetting her sexual appetite, making her near delirious in her need to act the wanton, fling herself on him, beg him to make love to her, and hope to hell she didn't freeze up on him again.

Not that she felt like freezing, not one little bit, she recognised dizzily as they threaded slowly through the narrow, ancient streets. The playful breeze was warm and she could smell the sea, and the river, and the orange trees that seemed to be planted everywhere.

She belonged here; she really did. It made her feel so happy. This place, and being here with him, intoxicated her far more than the wine had done.

'I'd forgotten how relaxing this corner of Spain

could be,' she said on a breathy little sigh, and dropped her glossy chestnut head against his powerful shoulder.

'Andalusia? Or the best part of a bottle of wine?' he queried dryly, slipping an arm around her waist for greater support. 'Not long now; almost home.'

Home. Oh, it sounded so good! Far too good to be true. A tear formed in the corner of each eye. If only they could have spent their married life here, away from...

'Whoops!' She stumbled over an uneven cobblestone and the momentary plunge into misery was forgotten as Roman, with a darkly muttered imprecation, swept her up into his arms and carried her the rest of the short distance and then beneath the stone portal of the house.

'You didn't carry me over the threshold on our honeymoon,' she murmured, knowing her words were all slurring together in a way that made her want to giggle irrepressibly.

And it wasn't really the effects of alcohol, either. It was being held in his arms, pressed against that gorgeous, macho male body, her arms clinging around his neck, her face so very close to his. Definitely close enough to kiss...

'We had an audience, remember?' he answered lightly, as if he were trying to humour a difficult child. 'You were such a timid little thing, I didn't want to embarrass you. The slightest thing made your face turn into a beetroot and sent you scurrying for cover.'

He had a point, she conceded. Three years ago she'd been a pathetic wimp. She responded airily, 'I remember. All the staff gathered to give the master's new bride the once-over. Staring, picking me to pieces!'

She felt his whole body tense, the arms that held her turning to steel bars. She wound her arms more tightly around his neck. Hey ho! What did the past matter? They were alone now; that was the important thing. No old family retainers to exclaim over the total unsuitability of *el patrón*'s new wife, as she'd had no doubt they had done in the privacy of their own quarters.

Not that that sort of thing would bother her now, of course. Suddenly, she felt liberated, her own woman, capable of facing anyone and anything. Best of all, she wasn't afraid of disappointing Roman in bed. What she didn't know he could teach her. She would be a willing pupil!

'You get some strange ideas.' His long stride carried him across the cool, dimly lit hall. 'But then I never had the privilege of knowing what was going on inside your head.'

Because he hadn't asked? Or because she hadn't told him? Were they equally to blame for the complete lack of communication between them?

Cassie was in no fit state to come up with an answer to that; she was simply a mass of sensation, minus a brain. Her blood was singing through her veins, red-hot, burning her up. She'd expected him to put her down but he didn't. He carried her up the stairs as if she weighed no more than a kitten.

Tonight wasn't going to be a problem. Tonight she was more ready for him than she could ever have dreamed possible.

The fiendish bargain he'd struck had seemed like a violation of the worst possible kind. Until tonight. Tonight, making love with her husband—whole-heartedly responding to his incredible, overpowering, fantastic masculinity—was nothing short of natural, totally and overwhelmingly right.

She gave a long sigh of blissful anticipation as he paced his way to the side of the sumptuous bed by the light of the moon that slanted through the louvres, and slid her down to her feet, flicking on the bedside lamp at the same time.

Her arms still looped around his neck, Cassie stared up into the strong planes of his heartstoppingly arresting features and electrifying, bone-melting ex-citement made her sway on her feet, her breath com-ing rapidly, shallowly.

She tried to say his name but her mouth couldn't form the word; her lips parted uselessly. Ever since they'd arrived here this morning she'd been more and more sexually aware of him, trying to deny it because she hadn't wanted a repeat performance of their wed-ding night.

She knew now that wouldn't happen. During the last year she had finally grown up.

'*Por Dios!*' Roman muttered beneath his breath. Swiftly, he lifted his hands to remove hers from around his neck where her fingers had begun playing with the soft dark hairs at his nape.

Then, without any effort at all, he swung her round, found the zip at the back of her dress and pulled it down. The tiny rasping sound seemed unnaturally loud. Cassie held her breath, her heartbeats thudding wildly as deft fingers slid the fabric from her shoulders, down her arms, loosing the garment to let it pool at her feet.

Her need for him was so hot and heavy now, she could barely stand.

When he unclipped the back fastening of her bra and released her throbbing breasts Cassie felt she might expire on the spot from the wild clamour of sexual excitement, and a husky moan was dredged from deep inside her when he slid her brief black lace panties down the length of her trembling legs.

She made to turn, her mouth running dry, wanting to undress him, to touch her nakedness to his, but he propelled her forward with one firm hand, the other pulling down the thin, silky bed-sheet.

'Sleep it off, Cass,' he advised grimly. 'You obviously decided to get drunk—' he laid cruel emphasis on the word '—to help you through the night. Well, I've got news for you, *mi esposa*. I find that a definite turn-off.'

He marched back to the door, then paused, his tone dry, 'I'll join you later, if only to make sure you don't raid the wine cellar for more Dutch courage. But, never fear, I won't touch you. So sleep well.'

CHAPTER SEVEN

CASSIE stirred fretfully and came awake. And wished she hadn't. Asleep, she didn't have to relive the scene of her humiliation, the way her red-hot anticipation of the night ahead had been so effectively doused by the ice of his parting words.

Drunk.

It was still only the middle of the night and the room was in total darkness. She'd been too busy crying herself to sleep to think about anything practical, like turning off the bedside lamp.

Roman must have done it.

For the first time amid the internal racket of her clamouring waking thoughts she heard the sound of his breathing. And held her own breath, her naked body going tense beneath the fine silky sheet.

He had joined her. He had said he would.

But the bed was huge and he was lying as far away from her as he could get without falling off the edge.

He had said he wouldn't touch her.

Because he believed she'd deliberately got drunk so that when it came to keeping her side of his Machiavellian bargain she would be too fuddled to take any notice of what was going on! Well, it had sort of started off that way, she admitted honestly, but somewhere along the line it had changed.

Quite when she had realised that she still loved her husband, always had and always would, she couldn't really recall.

It hadn't hit her like a bolt of lightning, but had been gradually unfurling inside her, like the newly opening petals of a rose, becoming more certain with every breath she took.

She loved him so.

Her heart leapt, twisted, and ended up somewhere in her throat.

Her life with Roman, before she'd gathered enough courage to leave him, had been liberally spattered with mistakes. Far too many mistakes, the greatest of which had been her inability to communicate with him and explain her feelings.

Never again!

Whatever the future held—and as far as she knew he wasn't looking beyond three months—she owed it to both of them to be open and honest. Starting with telling him that if she'd given the impression that she was about to sink into an alcoholic heap, it had only been because the thought of spending the night with him had intoxicated her!

She hoisted herself up on one elbow, gingerly narrowing the distance between them. Her eyes were growing more accustomed to the darkness now and she could see the outline of his dark, beautifully shaped head against the white pillow. The sheet was tangled around his hips, and the shadowy sweep of his tautly muscled back was a temptation too far.

Her heart lurching, her mouth running dry, she reached out a hand and touched him. Just gently. From the warm nape of his neck her fingers slipped between his shoulder blades, loving the warmth of his skin, the slick texture, and down, down the ridge of vertebrae, sliding across to the hard prominence of his hipbone, exploring him as she had never dared to do before.

The arm he wasn't lying on was flung upwards, covering his face, giving her tenderly roving fingers access to the lower part of his chest. And lower, trailing down the washboard flatness of his stomach, her fingers stilling as they tangled in crisp, thick body hair.

Her heart was beating wildly, clamouring beneath her breast, her breathing difficult to regulate. She could touch him if she wanted to, and she did want to, but it would be an invasion of his personal privacy, wouldn't it? While he was asleep?

Forcing her hand to stay quietly and exactly where it was, she pulled in a ragged breath and bent forward to put her lips against the oiled satin skin of his shoulder, her throbbing, almost painfully aroused breasts meeting the hard plane of his back.

She wriggled against him, pressing closer; she couldn't help it. Her mind had gone on holiday and she was acting on instinctive, primitive need. Being so breathtakingly close to him, skin to burning skin, felt so right, so natural. She couldn't begin to imagine why she'd ever been unable to respond to him.

A small mew of pleasure escaped her throat, her whole body so sensitised now she knew she was about to wrap herself round him, make him wake, force him to bring her the release that only he could give.

But if he didn't want to give it?

The thought cooled her like a dash of icy water. If he rejected her, as she had formerly rejected him, pushing him away whenever he came near her after the awkwardness of their wedding night, she would be utterly devastated, humiliated...

She sucked in a savagely painful hiss of breath, realising for the very first time exactly how he must have felt and why, after a time, he had stayed away from her so often.

Sudden tears burned behind her eyes. How could she have done that to him when she'd been so much in love with him? How could she have been so self-centred, never giving a thought to how he must have felt, absorbed in her own immature hang-ups?

A tear of bitter regret fell on his shoulder blade. Unthinkingly, she bent her head and lapped it away with the tip of her tongue. And heard him moan softly, deep in his throat.

Awake? For how long? When had the rhythm of his breathing altered, become shallower, more rapid? Cassie's body went still. Waiting. Tense with the dread of having the tables turned on her. And he said, his voice husky with need, 'Touch me, Cass.'

Relief drenched through her. He wasn't going to take his revenge by telling her to keep her hands to herself. Relief and something stronger, wilder, had her pressing her naked body to his, fitting her thighs beneath his, her hand dipping lower.

Fully aroused, he was sensational. She shuddered with deep, spiralling ecstasy, her head spinning wildly as he groaned raggedly and swept round towards her, crushing her in his arms, parting her legs with a strong hair-roughened thigh.

'Wait—' She freed her trapped hand and raised it to gently touch his face, the heel of her palm resting along his tough, stubbly jawline, her fingers against one jutting cheekbone. 'I want to tell you—I promise you it wasn't just that I'd had a bit too much to drink. It was the thought of tonight that intoxicated me...'

If he believed her, he didn't say so. But perhaps the way his mouth took hers was answer enough. The hungry mastery of his kiss made her feel as if she were drowning; the hands that caressed and tormented every inch of her body sent her into a state of delirium and there were no words spoken when he finally plunged into her willing, receptive body.

But who needed words when two desperately needy bodies, two loving souls were communing in the darkness of the warm, sweetly scented Spanish night?

'If I didn't know better, I'd say you were not the woman I married.' Roman's slightly accented voice was soft and sultry and Cassie smiled dreamily into his smoky eyes.

The tone of his voice told her that he liked the woman she had become in his bed far better than the woman he had married. She wasn't going to spoil the magic they'd created together by reminding him of why he'd chosen an immature, biddable little thing to be his wife.

Around dawn they'd fallen asleep in each other's arms and, moments ago, his light kisses on her eyelids had woken her. Last night had been spectacular; they hadn't been able to get enough of each other, like starving people suddenly coming across a banquet.

Untutored as she was, her responses to him had surprised her. She'd been quite shameless, very much more than merely willing, wanting to give to him as much as he had given to her.

'Same beautiful hair,' he murmured, running his fingers through the long silky strands that were splayed out over the pillow, burnished to copper by the sunlight that filtered through the partly opened louvres. 'Same eyes—like the finest topaz—but with a light behind them that was never there before.'

The tips of his fingers slid across her cheek, found her parted lips and she reached up, looping her hands behind his head, pulling him down to her, and the kiss was like a drug, sending her spinning out of control and when he broke it she gave a tiny sob of denial.

'Shh—' he murmured, his eyes wicked, his sultry

mouth curving. 'Patience, *mi esposa*. I have not yet finished my inventory. Indulge me.'

She placed a shaky hand on his broad, bronzed chest, her body trembling with sharp awareness, her voice thick as she protested, 'Do you like tormenting me?'

'I love it.' His sensual mouth framed the words softly, liquid grey eyes gleaming beneath the thick black lashes. 'Almost as much as I love touching you, looking at you. Cassie, *mia*, you have matured beautifully.'

A languid hand slid the silk sheet away from her body. 'Lie back for me; let me look at you,' he commanded lazily as his hands swept over her engorged breasts, over her slender waist, following the feminine flare of her hips, then trailing inwards, to the apex of her thighs. Cassie reached for him, writhing with the burning fever of desire, parting her legs in wanton invitation, glorying in the release of knowing her feeble hang-ups were a thing of the past, that she could at last show him how much she loved him.

Then briefly, like a shadow, she saw a frown gather between his eyes, his jawline tightening as he pulled in his breath.

Something was wrong. Hadn't she pleased him as much as she'd thought she had? Despite what he'd just said, did he suddenly find her eagerness distasteful? Anxiety clouded Cassie's eyes as she lifted a tentative hand and laid it against the side of his face.

'Roman?'

At her touch, the sound of her voice, the frown

disappeared and the stillness that had held his body rigid melted away. She saw dark colour streak his hard, jutting cheekbones as he gave a rough growl low in his throat and demonstrated the full power of his possession.

She hadn't known it could be like this, Cassie mused one hour later as they exited the shower, wrapped around each other. The physical expression of love was so addictive.

She felt so sated she could barely move, and closed her eyes as he reached for a fluffy bath sheet and gently patted her dry before mopping the moisture from his own superb body. Thankfully, whatever had briefly troubled him had been forgotten. Or perhaps she had simply imagined it…

'The day is half gone,' he told her as he rubbed the towel over his hair, leaving it sticking up in endearing spikes. 'What would you like to do with the rest of it? Take a picnic to the beach? Or perhaps you'd prefer a restaurant?'

'I'd rather stay here,' she admitted huskily, her golden eyes drenched with soft emotion.

Roman grinned at her, his teeth very white against the bronze tones of his skin, his eyes glinting wickedly. 'I hoped you'd say that. Far more interesting things can happen in the privacy of our own home.' He dropped the towel, closed the small gap between them and put a brief kiss across her mouth. 'I'll make coffee and find something to eat. Come down when you're ready. And Cass—' he was already at the door to their adjoining bedroom '—wear something easy to get out of!'

Waves of love rolled over her, making her giddy. She wanted to stay here with him for ever, just the two of them.

Just the two? She suddenly remembered that she'd forgotten to take her pill last night. They might already be a threesome! She couldn't recall how many times they'd made love.

But it didn't matter, did it? Surely now that the lovemaking side of their marriage had been put so magnificently right he would want her to stay, want to make their marriage work? He had never pretended to be in love with her, but after last night he would put their troubled past behind him and build on what they now had.

Of course he would!

And even if he didn't love her now, love could grow, couldn't it?

Rough-drying her hair with the towel he'd discarded, she wandered through to the bedroom, the prickle of excitement deep inside her beginning all over again as she wondered which of her many new garments would be the most flattering and the simplest to remove!

CHAPTER EIGHT

'YOU are certainly a different person now,' Roman commented smoothly. He looked at ease, one arm draped along the back of the bench seat, his fingers touching the tousled copper strands of her hair as it tumbled over her shoulders. But his relaxed smile didn't reach eyes that seemed, in the half-light of a misty dawn, strangely wary. 'Is it the year away from me, from Spain, that has made you so? Being back in England has made you happier?'

Cassie glanced quickly away, swung her legs up on the upholstered bench seat that hugged the far side of the rose-smothered summer house and leant back against him.

She really didn't want to think about that year of separation, or the two years that had gone before. What had started out as a cold-blooded, wicked bargain had turned into a truly wonderful second honeymoon. She didn't want anything to spoil it.

Five weeks of wedded bliss, of lazy sun-drenched days, velvet, perfumed nights, wild bursts of passion in the most unexpected places, at the most unexpected times—lovers getting to know every intimate detail of each other's bodies in their own secluded paradise. Being shut away from the outside world had left her feeling she inhabited a haven of magical unreality.

But unfortunately reality was about to poke its nose in, she conceded reluctantly. Of course he would want to know why she'd walked out on their marriage. Only by raking over the past could they hope to put the future right. And if she looked reality squarely and bravely in the face she would have to admit that she still didn't know whether he wanted her to stay with him beyond the three-month limit he'd set.

And she was almost certain she was pregnant.

She dragged a sigh up from the bottom of her lungs. The cold breath of reality was definitely uncomfortable.

Roman said, his voice controlled, 'It is a subject that interests me, even if you would prefer not to think about our misguided marriage.'

'Misguided?' she echoed tremulously. After these last rapturous weeks, did he still think their marriage had been a mistake? How could that be, when they had become so close? Physically, at least, though there had been times when she'd been sure something was troubling him.

He snatched in an impatient breath. 'Look at me when I'm talking to you!' he commanded gruffly, placing strong hands on her hips and swinging her round so that her feet hit the tiled floor and she was slewed across the cushions, facing him.

Cassie could feel his anger and it made her want to weep. Something was wrong, very wrong, and she had to face it, not keep brushing it under the carpet, pretending it was all in her imagination. She asked, as calmly as she could, 'Roman, what's on your mind? Something is.' She met his brooding eyes, trying not to show her anxiety, her very real fear. 'We've been happy together, you know we have, yet there have been times when you've seemed to distance yourself...times when you've looked at me with something like disgust. I want to know why.'

He gave her a lancing look, his mouth tight round the words that suddenly poured from him. 'When we first married I thought I could make you content—happy, even. But after our wedding night together it became painfully obvious that I couldn't. You couldn't bear it when I touched you. Now it seems you can't get enough of sex,' he uttered darkly. 'So who taught you? You certainly didn't allow me that privilege.'

'Oh!' She felt her face burn with sudden outraged colour. How could he think such a thing, let alone say it? The morning sun was beginning to break through the mist, the air shimmering with opaline colours; outside the summer house, a stand of eucalyptus trees swayed gracefully in the slight breeze, their misty white branches and silver leaves ghostly in the growing light. But inside it was darker, Roman's face shadowed and suddenly somehow forbidding.

A shudder rocked her body.

'You are cold? Or have I touched a nerve?' Roman asked drily.

'Not cold, angry,' she framed vehemently. 'How could you think that of me, after the way we've been together? I don't sleep around! You're the only man I've ever made love with!'

Even though she was only wearing a pair of brief turquoise cotton shorts and a matching bra-style top, the morning was warm. Too warm, really. She felt a band of perspiration form above her short upper lip and saw by the tightening of his mobile, utterly sensuous mouth that her instinctive and truthful reply hadn't impressed him.

He believed his assumption was the correct one, that since leaving him she'd been indulging in multiple affairs. And was he jealous? Roman, jealous! She squashed the surge of hope very decisively. Letting herself believe that her husband really did love her could be dangerous, could lead to a disappointment that would be almost impossible to bear.

'Why are you asking all this? Why now?' she asked dully, hopelessness dousing all that vehement anger as she at last understood the insulting reality of what had been troubling him.

Was everything about to end? It certainly looked that way, especially since he obviously didn't believe her assertion that she hadn't been with any other man.

For the first time since they'd been back together they hadn't instinctively turned to each other, making love until the sun burned holes in the sea mist, taking it in turns to fetch breakfast in bed. This morning the kiss that had woken her had been perfunctory, but his suggestion that they take their coffee down to the summer house hadn't bothered her. Not until now. Was he already tiring of her, as had once been stringently prophesised? Was his stubborn belief that she'd been unfaithful the excuse he was looking for?

Cassie hugged her arms around her midriff, shaking inside now. Everything seemed spoiled, about to fall apart. 'Leaving aside your insulting remarks about my supposed promiscuity, I thought we'd—' she lifted her slender shoulders in a hopeless gesture '—we'd settled our differences.'

'With sex? I think not.' The white shirt he was wearing gleamed in a sudden shaft of sunlight. Impressive shoulders lifted in a dismissive shrug. 'I admit that at first I found your unexpected response to me astonishing, and, being a normal male, I delighted in your sexual generosity. But that was the froth, was it not? It is what's beneath the surface that interests me.'

Male lust—was this Roman's way of warning her that mere lust was what the last five weeks had been about? Cassie pondered miserably. She was a hundred per cent thankful that she hadn't let herself hope that he was learning to love her. Well, she hadn't, not really.

She didn't know what he wanted to hear her say, but at least he was giving her a little breathing space as he bent over the coffee tray on the low table, pouring from the silver pot, sugaring hers.

Lost in disquieting thoughts, unprepared for his

next question, she gave a shocked gasp as he asked levelly, 'Tell me, did you marry me for money?'

'What put that in your head?' she demanded when she could get her mouth to frame the words. 'So I'm a gold-digger now, as well as a slut!'

'It was suggested. Before our marriage.'

'Who by?' she spluttered hotly. 'One of your aunts, at a guess—neither of them liked me!'

'I refused to believe it at the time,' he stated, as if she hadn't spoken. 'You were sweet, unspoiled; you didn't demand designer dresses or fancy jewels—the exact opposite of the society creatures I was used to having pushed under my nose. I had a hard enough time persuading you to let me buy your wedding dress and a suitable trousseau. Do you remember?'

Of course she remembered! He'd already discharged those of her father's debts that the sale of the house hadn't covered, and she hadn't wanted to be a further drain on him, even if he could well afford it.

She and Roy hadn't had much, but they could have pooled their resources. She could have kitted herself out with something his exalted family wouldn't have been too ashamed to see her wearing. But, no, even that amount of independence had been denied her!

'So what changed your mind?' she demanded furiously. If he wanted a fight, he could have one, even if the thought of being at odds with him tore her apart. 'Just when have I ever asked you for money?'

'Our wedding night, and the years that followed,'

he answered flatly. 'That changed my mind. You weren't interested in me as a husband, the father of your children. You were free of those debts you felt morally bound to discharge, and as soon as enough time had passed for you to be sure your brother was settled, drawing a healthy salary, you ran away, informing me that you'd be suing for divorce. I did wonder then if laying your hands on a hefty chunk of alimony had been your intention all along.'

He spread his hands expressively. 'What else was I to think? It was the only explanation that made any kind of sense. And of course,' he added with a dryness that sent a shaft of pain through her heart, 'the only reason you are here with me now, allowing me to use your body, comes down to money—stolen money.'

That he should think her a mercenary little gold-digger incensed her, but she clamped her soft lips together and forced back the blistering words she wanted to throw at him. He did have a point.

And now, if nothing else came of their time together, he had to hear her side of the story.

'I was *never* interested in your money,' she told him shortly. 'I was grateful when you offered to pay the outstanding debts—especially when you insisted that the sum involved represented no more to you than the loose change in your pocket. It meant that the remaining creditors didn't have to suffer—that Roy and I wouldn't have to live on the breadline, taking what jobs we could get to pay off the rest of the debts. So I guess, where that was concerned, I took the easy way out.

'But,' she emphasised firmly, 'if I hadn't been madly in love with you I would never have married you. Roy and I would have gone back to England and found some kind of work.' She gave him a fierce glare. If he was worried she might demand half his wretched estate, then she could put him out of his misery.

These last few weeks together had meant nothing to him, apart from fantastic sex—which was probably already beginning to bore him.

Been there, done that!

Otherwise why would he be trying to pick a fight, as good as accusing her of marrying him for his money?

'I have no intention of asking for a single peseta on our divorce!'

Why was she talking of divorce when for the past few weeks she'd been hoping that their marriage was mended? she groaned silently. The knot of misery behind her breastbone tightened, spread down into her stomach. She felt distinctly queasy. And she knew the answer to her own question. Of course she did. He wouldn't be throwing these vile accusations at her if he wanted their marriage to continue.

She stumbled to her feet. Everything was going wrong. When they'd wandered down through the gardens this morning everything had been touched with magic, and now—

A commanding hand closed around her wrist, halt-

ing her attempts at a dignified flight, edging her back
onto the seat beside him.

'You said, and I quote, that you were "madly in
love" with me when we married—I believe you are
lying because I saw no evidence of it.'

It was an accusation; of course it was. But gently
said. His fingers slid away from her wrist. Meaning
she was free to go now he'd made his point?
Meaning she could defend herself or not? That he
was indifferent?

Any moment now she would burst into tears and
humiliate herself. She could feel her lungs tremble,
the pressure building up in her throat and behind her
eyes. But she wasn't going to let it happen.

'You already know the truth, Roman. But I'll re-
fresh your memory.' The words emerged more acidly
than she'd intended. Deliberately, she pulled in a
slow breath and softened her tone. 'When we married, I was an anachronism—a nineteenth-century
woman living in the late twentieth. I was brought up
by a domineering father, convent-educated, and had
no experience of men—barring Father, Roy, and
Cindy's brother, of course. Father thought females
were put on this earth to be of use to males, and for
no other reason.'

She took a gulp of hot coffee and replaced the cup
with a clatter that threatened to break the saucer.
'When I left school at eighteen, he used the strength
of his character, plus a large dollop of emotional
blackmail, to convince me it was my duty to stay
home and replace the part-time housekeeper he'd had

to employ after Mum died. So when I met you, fell in love, my self-confidence was already about floor level. I'd fallen for you in a big way, but I knew you were way out of my league—wealthy, sophisticated, oozing with self-confidence. Everything I wasn't.'

But she'd married him anyway, because she'd been so in love with him it had hurt. She'd known he hadn't loved her, but she'd had his affection, and that had seemed very much better than having any other man's doting adoration.

'So I was the object of a rather belated juvenile infatuation.' He dismissed the love that had swamped her life with a tired smile. 'What went wrong? I did everything possible to see that you were comfortable, free from anxieties. Did I not try to ease you into your new role, your new lifestyle?'

'Ease?' she scorned. 'Leaving me with your mother and the aunts while you flew to England—?'

'It was for the best,' Roman said bluntly. 'I had to sort out the financial mess your father had left behind. Seeing the family home sold up, dealing with lawyers and creditors would have upset you unnecessarily. It was far more important that you got to know my family—your new family—better, acclimatised yourself, began arrangements for our wedding. So please don't try to accuse me of doing the wrong thing.'

'No? You acted exactly as my father would have done. Arrogantly,' she derided. 'And don't look so affronted! I may have been unable to voice any opinion three years ago, but I can now! *You* decided what

was *best* for me without asking me what *I* wanted. I
was so well conditioned that I never even thought of
objecting. I did as I was told to do. And suffered for
it. By the time we were married I had been thoroughly brainwashed. I was nowhere good enough for
you.' She ticked off on her fingers, her voice tight
with the memory of how humiliated she'd been made
to feel. 'I was a foreigner, had no breeding, no
money, no looks to speak of. You, naturally, were
the cat's flaming whiskers! But you were being typ-
ically difficult, only marrying me to spite your family. You were highly sexed and experienced; I would
very soon bore you. As soon as I'd given you the
heir the estate needed, I'd be pensioned off, hidden
away.'

His stillness following her heated, heartfelt outburst emanated tension. His eyes looked black and
chillingly cold and his voice was low and dangerous
as he asked, 'Who said these things?'

'Does it matter now?' She suddenly felt empty,
drained, as if a light had gone out inside her.
Recalling those earlier, desperate insecurities, and
how they'd been fostered—no doubt with the intention of making her call the wedding off—had reminded her that they were indeed worlds apart, in
culture, social standing, everything; the past few
weeks had been nothing but a fantasy, a foolish
dream.

'It matters. *Tell* me.'

As forceful as ever, she thought defeatedly. Well,
what the heck? The women of his family hadn't

earned her loyalty. He probably wouldn't believe her, anyway. He'd already accused her of marrying him for his money and of sleeping around during their separation. Calling her a liar as well wouldn't make a whole lot of difference.

'Your aunts,' she said shortly. 'To give her her due, your mother didn't take part in those intimate family discussions—she made her point by being rather chillingly polite.'

'*Por Dios!*' He shot to his feet, his wide shoulders rigid, the now bright sunlight accentuating the hard lines of his face. 'You were *my* choice—how dared they?' he growled.

Cassie shivered. Roman in a temper was a sight to behold, brooding eyes glowering, his hands bunched into savage-looking fists, tucked hard against the sides of his long lean legs.

But at least he hadn't called her a liar or accused her of impugning his exalted family. That thought took root, warmed her a little and then blossomed sweetly as he held out a hand to her, his voice soft when he said, 'Come here.'

She went. Well, wouldn't she always? His arms enfolded her and she leant her head against the angle of his shoulder, her heart lurching with the love she could no more banish than fly as he murmured, 'I begin to understand a little. By the time we got to our wedding night, what little confidence you'd had in yourself had been well and truly shattered. Faced with an experienced bridegroom who was supposedly prepared to hide you away and pension you off when you'd done your duty and provided the estate with an heir, you froze.

'Naturally, you didn't want to make love with me because it could lead to a pregnancy, and you didn't want to spend the rest of your life hidden away, closely chaperoned by the females who had already made you feel unwanted.'

He sounded almost smug, Cassie thought with a weak smile, and he was patting her back as if she were a lap dog in need of quieting. Never mind all those earlier unpleasant accusations, being held in his arms was having the usual effect. She couldn't fight the way her body now needed his so desperately.

'You should have told me all this at the time,' he chided gently. 'I could then have put your fears at rest.' A final comforting pat and his hands slid up to her shoulders, holding her away from him. 'But you always did seem tongue-tied around me, though you could chatter nineteen to the dozen with Cindy and her brother. It is a pity that you were so in awe of me. A few words of explanation would have made all the difference.'

Spoken like a true feudal overlord—a Spanish one at that. Lofty, patronising. He was back to treating her like a silly child without an atom of sense in her head or an opinion worth listening to.

At one time she would have meekly agreed with anything he said. She'd been brought up to believe that men were superior beings, that they always knew best.

Now she tipped back her head. 'Pregnant or not,

I was pretty effectively hidden away, wasn't I? Besides...' She gave him a radiant smile to soften the criticism. Being held by him was giving her the confidence she needed to delve into the past, display all her earlier failings. And maybe, in doing so, she could convince him she wasn't the promiscuous madam he'd accused her of being. 'I would never have married you if I'd thought I'd get put in a cupboard and locked away as soon as I gave birth to your heir. I knew you weren't cruel. It was...' She splayed her hands out against his chest, feeling his body heat, the heavy thud of his heartbeats beneath the soft white silk.

She wanted to move closer, very much closer, but that must wait. Already the closeness of him was making her tremble, making her heart race. 'I'd been told you were highly sexed, experienced,' she went on shakily, her breath coming raggedly. 'Your aunts were at pains to mention your affairs—models, dancers, all beautiful. Not for marrying, of course, but necessary for a young man, provided discretion was observed.'

She moved closer, fitting her body to his. She was so hungry for him; surely he knew that now? Surely he would understand?

She felt the tug of his breath just before he abruptly moved away, and anxiety peaked her brows as she said to his rigidly held back, 'Roman—I was a virgin, and, worse than that, I'd never had a proper boyfriend. I was afraid of disappointing you. The fear stuck in my head and I couldn't get it out. Do you understand? I kept thinking you'd compare me with those others—the beautiful, experienced ones who knew how to please a man.'

Why wouldn't he turn and look at her? Why?

'That first night fear of disappointing you made me freeze. I knew—knew—' She was beginning to stumble over her words; the ungiving rigidity of his spine and the way he was holding his head was turning her back into the tongue-tied wretch she had been before.

She gathered herself and said more firmly, 'I knew you didn't love me—you'd picked me because I'd make no demands on you that you wouldn't be happy to meet. But you did have affection for me, and I thought that would be enough. It wasn't, though,' she confirmed bleakly. 'If you'd loved me I'd have been able to tell you how I felt. If you'd loved me you wouldn't have been comparing me to those others; you would have taught me how to respond, taken away the fear. But I knew you weren't in love with me and I was too ashamed of myself to explain. I just pushed you away whenever you came near. I couldn't face more humiliation.'

Silence. Just the soft call of a dove, the lazy rustle of light wind in the trees. Her throat went tight. Was he turning her words over in his mind, testing them for validity?

'Say something,' she begged thickly. He did turn then, and what she saw in his eyes pushed her breath back into her lungs.

Regret? Sadness? How could she be sure?

'Then I must accept the larger part of the blame,' he said stiffly. She had never heard him sound quite so Spanish. He withdrew his hands from the side pockets of the tailored grey chinos he was wearing and glanced at his watch. His eyes were blank as he imparted coolly, 'When you left me my first instinct was to get over to England and drag you back.'

He was speaking slowly, that sexy accent more marked than usual, as if he were carefully picking his words. Cassie couldn't believe he hadn't been only too happy to see the back of his unsatisfactory wife.

'Why would you have wanted to do that?'

He acknowledged the incredulity of her tone with a slight dip of his dark, breathtakingly handsome head. 'Why? Because you were mine.'

And Roman Fernandez didn't relinquish his possessions easily—not even when they were worthless, she acknowledged mutely. 'So why didn't you follow me?'

Would she have returned to Spain with him? Perhaps. During those first few weeks back in England she'd been a mess. She had destroyed her marriage before it had started. She had loathed herself. If he had come for her, demanding her return, she would have gone, hoping that by some miracle things would improve.

But he hadn't come—had made no attempt to contact her—and she'd known she was on her own, had to make a life for herself.

'I changed my mind.' Another restless glance at

his watch. He seemed to be avoiding her eyes, as if he again wished to distance himself from her. 'You were, to put it mildly, very immature. Not in a giggly, schoolgirl way—that would never have attracted me to you—but lacking in a sense of who you were. Introverted and insecure. I believed that having to stand on your own two feet for a while—be entirely responsible for your own well-being, without a father or a husband to tell you what to do—would allow you to grow up.'

If his eyes were suddenly hard, his voice was even more so, 'And I was right. You grew up with a vengeance, *mi esposa*. Certainly, you have no more fear of sex. I have ample evidence of that. The only thing I do not know—or wish to know—is who tutored you so thoroughly.'

CHAPTER NINE

'ROMAN!'

But he was already walking rapidly away, striding along the winding path that led back towards the house, his feet brushing the bordering lavender plants, releasing the sweetly astringent perfume into the sparkling air. If he'd heard her anguished cry he gave no sign of it.

Casting an agitated glance at the coffee tray, Cassie decided to come back for it later. It seemed pretty hopeless, but she had to make another attempt to convince him that no way had she been sleeping around during their year apart. He was the only man she had made love with, or wanted to be with.

She caught up with him as he entered the courtyard through the arched doorway in the stone wall. Her heart was pounding and she knew her face had turned a fiery, anxious red.

'Roman—wait!'

In complete contrast he was cool, composed. She had never seen him look so solemn. One dark brow lifted slightly in silent enquiry as he glanced down into her troubled features.

'I want to talk—and I want you to listen.' Her tongue felt too big for her mouth. Would she ever be able to make him believe she hadn't been tutored in the art of pleasing a man in bed by a string of experts? The subject had obviously been troubling him for the last five weeks and now he couldn't get it out of his head.

'The talking has been done, *querida*,' he intoned with a bleak finality that cut deep into her soul, his beautiful smoky eyes devoid of all expression. 'It was cathartic but necessary, you understand. The last few weeks have been—' wide shoulders drifted eloquently upwards '—what can I say? A dream. But always one must wake and face reality. We had to discover why our marriage had been such...' He paused, as if searching for a word that wouldn't be too hurtful. 'So uncomfortable. Now—' again that infuriating, frustrating glance at his watch '—I'm expected in Seville for a business meeting later this morning. I shall be away for two days. We will talk again on my return. Not of the past, but of the future.'

Take me with you! she wanted to plead. But didn't. She felt as if she'd been hit with a brick. He had spoken as if he had every intention of giving her the divorce she'd asked for a year ago and the old pattern was repeating itself. Business trips taking him away for longer and longer periods. Always leaving her behind.

Yet it *had* been different this time, she told herself wildly. This time their coming together had been gloriously successful; they'd been like two halves of a whole, blissfully inseparable. Did that, in the end, count for nothing?

As the cool silence of the house swallowed him, she sank onto a stone bench in the courtyard and listened to the cool music of the fountain, breathing the scent of the sweetly perfumed oleanders into labouring lungs, doing her very best to calm down. A divorce was the very last thing she wanted. She loved him so much.

He'd asked questions and she'd answered them as honestly as she knew how. His curiosity had been satisfied and he now knew why she had been forced to leave him, why their marriage had been such a failure to begin with.

That his conclusions were the wrong ones simply wouldn't occur to him. The past lived. The mistakes hadn't been erased, and a new and equally devastating misconception—that she'd been sleeping with other men—had been born. His whole attitude told her that he was set on continuing what she had started—the ending of their marriage.

The mental pain was so overwhelming she didn't know how she was ever going to be able to cope with it. And when, minutes later, he stood over her, she looked at him blankly, the sparkle blanketed from her eyes beneath the weight of her misery.

He looked cool and fresh, and she could smell the tangy cologne he always wore, a scent that would live in her memory for ever. His car keys were in one hand, a slim overnight case in the other.

He said levelly, 'I've recalled Manuel and Teresa;

they should be here within the hour. After our less than wholehearted attention, the house and the garden need some supervision,' he explained, dauntingly practical and chillingly cool.

Cassie shivered. So the second honeymoon was well and truly over. Her heart was hurting and her mind felt as if someone had ripped it apart and flung the ragged pieces to the four winds. Useless to ask him to listen to what she wanted to say while she was in this state. He wouldn't welcome near-hysterical protestations of innocence or tearful pleas to take her back on a permanent basis.

Besides, she didn't want to come over as a gibbering wreck. She needed time to wind down, gather some control and come to terms with what had happened this morning. His absence would at least give her that.

'Fine.' She returned his glance as coolly as she could manage and turned away before he could see the tears that were brimming in her eyes. 'See you in two days. Take care.'

Ten minutes later Cassie was dressed in a cool cotton shift dress in clear lemon-yellow, comfy flat sandals with a floppy-brimmed straw sun hat covering her coiled-back hair. No way was she going to be here when the housekeeper and her gardener husband returned to take up their duties.

She needed to be on her own, away from the house where everything was a bittersweet reminder of Roman. She needed to think, to get herself together, face what looked like being the final breakdown of her marriage. She also had to discover whether there was any truth in what she was beginning to believe...

Out in the shade of the narrow street that wound down into the heart of the old town she gave a small sigh of relief, feeling marginally more in control of her emotions. Teresa, as she remembered the short but heftily built woman, was a bit of a martinet, ruling the seeming army of staff with a rod of iron, making sure *el patrón*'s slightest wish was anticipated, treating the unsuitable new bride with decidedly sniffy disdain.

That, Cassie decided, she could do without right now!

Her first port of call was the chemist in the main square, and as she tucked the package into the bottom of the straw bag that teamed with her hat and stepped out into the sizzling sunlight she gave a slight shiver.

Soon she would know, one way or the other.

Had she conceived Roman's child? Or had her periods gone back to being all over the place because she'd forgotten to take the pill on that first fateful, never-to-be-forgotten night?

But she wouldn't think about that right now, not when there was so much other stuff going on inside her head. She had taken the day to get her mind straightened out, not add to the muddle. She would think about the consequences of having conceived Roman's child when and if she knew for sure she had.

Nevertheless, she felt distinctly shaky inside as she

headed for one of the pavement cafés and sank down at a table beneath the shade of a huge striped umbrella. She ordered freshly squeezed orange juice with lots of ice and tried to make her mind a blank, watching the life of the ancient Spanish town pass by.

But it didn't work. Her mind was filled with one thought alone: Roman's child—how she would love it!

It was almost dusk when she returned to the great stone house that dominated the narrow street. Her hair had come adrift from the neat coil and tumbled riotously around her shoulders and the wind from the sea had whipped away her straw hat as she'd walked on the long sandy beach. She felt hot and sticky and her feet hurt.

But it had been worth it. Her mind had gradually cleared and she felt a million times more hopeful than when she had set out. Hopeful enough to greet Teresa with a confident smile as she entered the huge, marble paved hall and found the housekeeper waiting.

'Good evening, Teresa. I hope you and your husband have settled back in.' A skeleton staff now, where once there had been an army. Had Roman refused to make use of this lovely place since their disastrous first honeymoon?

'*Señora.*' If anything, the housekeeper's impressive girth had much increased since Cassie had last seen her, and her features were, as ever, stony with disapproval. 'You wish for supper?'

Cassie permitted herself a tiny wry smile at the martyred tone. Three years ago she would have shaken her head and scuttled away, not wanting to be a nuisance. Now she said pleasantly, 'Please. Something light in the small *sala* in one hour. I need to shower and change.'

And do that test. Find out for sure if what she hoped with all her heart was true or just wishful thinking.

'*Sí, señora.* In one hour.' Was there a look of grudging approval in the older woman's small black eyes? Cassie couldn't be sure until the housekeeper said, a bit stiffly but nevertheless said, 'Welcome home. It has been too long,' and waddled away.

Sucking in a breath of pleased surprise Cassie flew up the great, curving staircase. Everything was going to be all right—it had to be! Teresa's acceptance of her had to be an omen. Didn't it?

But that was a minor thing. What really counted was the way she'd been able to go over the talk she and Roman had had this morning, rationally and calmly, picking up clues.

He had mentioned that he'd been attracted to her, that he hadn't wanted her to leave him, but had let her go for her own sake, allowing her time to become an adult woman who could stand on her own feet. And there had been no mistaking his anger when she'd confessed that his aunts had robbed her of what little self-confidence she'd had.

On his return they'd talk again. He had promised her that. Talk of the future. Their future together? The past had been dealt with, a necessary exercise but leaving him with that misconception over who else she'd been sleeping with.

She would try again to put that right. On that she was utterly determined.

Once that was out of the way—she permitted herself a dreamy, pleasurable sigh—there'd be no more pussy-footing around the subject. She'd come right out with it and ask him if he was willing to give their marriage a second chance.

She wanted to stay married to him. She needed him; it felt as if her whole life depended on it.

An hour later she floated down the stairs. She felt as if her feet were treading on air. She was carrying Roman's child within her body. She had never felt more blessed.

Today. If he kept to his word, Roman would be back today. Some time today.

Cassie paced the bedroom floor restlessly, too wound up with a mixture of excitement and apprehension to even try to relax. And it was only midday. It could be hours before he returned.

Oh, how she longed to see him again, to kiss him and touch him. To hold him close, will him to love her, just a little. A little would do for starters.

Hours of suspense, hours of waiting to discover whether she could finally make him believe that her supposed promiscuity was only in his mind, whether he'd be willing to take their marriage forward into the future.

And it was so hot. Airless. They were in for a storm, Manuel had said as she'd been helping him in the garden this morning—well, pottering, really, anything to pass the time until Roman's return. But she'd felt dizzy with the heat, the lack of sleep and lack of food. Her appetite had disappeared under the welter of growing emotions.

She'd already taken two cool showers. She was only wearing a half-cup white lace bra and the briefest of matching panties and she was still burning up with the oppressive heat.

Soon she'd have to dress. He might make it back by lunchtime. She wanted to be ready and waiting, looking her best. But what to wear?

She padded barefoot to the huge hanging cupboards and finally reached out a gossamer-fine floaty number patterned in soft swirls of cool blues and green. Her hands were shaking.

'Cass.'

The sound of his voice in the hot, sultry silence of the room startled her witless. She turned to face him, the light-as-air dress drifting from her fingers, pooling at her feet. She couldn't speak, not if her life had depended on it. Her heart was pounding roughly against her breastbone and her throat muscles had gone into spasm.

He was here, and now it was time to do what she'd promised herself. She'd get everything out into the open, tell him the truth—tell him she loved him and wanted to spend the rest of her life with him.

She wouldn't tell him about the baby, though. Not yet. He might look on it as emotional blackmail. He had to freely agree to keep their marriage going because he wanted it that way, not because he felt it was an inescapable duty.

Tentatively, she moistened her dry-as-dust lips and tried to swallow. Her throat still wouldn't work.

As soon as she could speak coherently, she would know whether he wanted her or not. Permanently. Her head began to spin dizzily as she watched him avidly. Scrub 'permanently', for the moment—she could tell he wanted her right now, if only for a brief hour of unreasoning rapture.

He'd closed the door behind him and had walked a couple of paces into the room. He looked tired. The lines of strain made his features harsher, but the dark smudges around his eyes didn't detract from the slow, simmering, brooding gaze that lingered over every lush curve of her scantily clad body.

Flesh burning, her stomach quivering, she instinctively raised her hands to him in mute supplication. He'd removed his jacket, dragged off his tie, dropping them on the floor, his eyes still riveted to her, a dull flush stealing over his hard cheekbones.

Slowly, his eyes lifted to hers, locking. She felt dizzy with longing, with needing him. Desperate. Her heart lurched. He wanted her, too—now. She knew he did. The truthful little speech she'd run over and over in her head evaporated in the sizzling heat of mutual desire.

With a tiny moan she ran towards him, her arms outstretched. Words were superfluous. What was needed was a whole lot of the sensuous lovemaking that they'd become so demonstrably good at. Together.

CHAPTER TEN

His eyes had turned to deepest smouldering silver, Cassie noted with a delirious kick of her heart as she impulsively wound her arms around his neck and wriggled her nearly naked body as close to his as she could possibly get.

She knew there were things she had to say to him, things she should tell him—plus the million-dollar question that had to be asked. But not now, not just yet... She needed this... Needed to feel close to him...

Her fingers tangled in the hair at his nape. It was damp with perspiration, the rest of it soft and ruffled, falling over his forehead in dark wayward strands, touching the clenched black bar of his brows.

His eyes were closed now, his mouth compressed. Cassie slid her hands down the strong column of his neck, splaying her fingers out over the intimidating width of his shoulders. He made no move to hold her but she knew he wanted to, that at any moment the power of her love for him would break through his resistance.

Her tingling breasts were pressed against the broad span of his chest and she could feel the heavy, rapid beat of his heart and the firm leap of his arousal against the yielding softness of her bare tummy, and that told her all she needed to know.

'I missed you,' she said, her voice thick with longing. She knew he wanted her, so why didn't he hold her? Why was he holding back, denying himself the reaffirmation of her love?

Her heart missing a beat, she slipped his shirt buttons from their moorings and slid her hands beneath the soft fabric, her palms moving frantically over the hot satin of his skin.

'So it would seem.' His voice was gritty, his eyes opening at last to spear her with silver intensity. 'As I've already said, the change in your attitude to sex is mind-blowing.'

'Don't!' She dropped her bright head, burrowing her face into his tautly muscled chest. 'This isn't just about sex,' she promised, the frenzied need to have him believe her making her slur her words. 'I know what you think of me, but don't! You mustn't—it simply isn't true!'

Any hope of coherency left her then; the warmth of his skin was burning her, the tangy, clean male scent of him drugging her senses. The power he had over her knocked her senseless, made her dizzy with a need that would never go away.

With a tiny smothered groan she pressed her mouth to his flat male nipple, tasting him recklessly, and dragged her hands over the hard arch of his ribcage and down over the tight muscles of his stomach and heard him pull air between his teeth just before he muttered, 'So be it!' and enfolded her, one hand pressing against the small of her back, pulling her closer into the thrusting power of him, the other tangling in the wild fall of her hair, dragging her head back.

'Por Dios!' The harsh words cut through the thick sultry silence as his mouth took hers with a raw passion that was almost savage. Cassie gave a cry of willing, exultant capitulation as his sensual mouth moulded hers, his tongue clashing with hers as he sought her inner sweetness.

Wild fingers tangled in the soft rich darkness of his hair, anchoring his head, holding him to her as if she would never let him go. And she wouldn't, not if she could help it. That was her last clear thought as his thighs thrust between the quivering shakiness of hers and he edged her back towards the bed.

Together they fell onto the soft silk that covered the deep mattress and he rolled over and pinned her beneath his weight, finding the front fastening of her bra with impatient fingers, releasing the lush fullness of her breasts to the urgency of his hungry hands.

Only then did he break the demand of his kiss, dipping his dark head to suckle her, and Cassie gasped out loud, flinging her arms above her head in wild and wanton abandon, his for the taking, now and always.

And then the phone rang.

It was the internal house phone. It sat on a small table beneath one of the tall windows. Roman's lithe body stiffened and Cassie wrapped her arms around his neck and held him. 'Ignore it,' she breathed raggedly.

But Roman reached for her clasped hands and released himself, swung his long legs over the side of the bed, dragged in a long shuddering breath then stalked across to the strident instrument.

Would he come back to her? Cassie wondered unhappily. His face in profile looked remote. Guarded. All passion gone. She knew—who better?—that he'd returned as full of reservations as he'd been when he'd left two days ago—but she'd broken through his defences, hadn't she? And in the sweet, lazy aftermath of loving she would have told him what he needed to know, pleaded with him if necessary to give her another chance to make their marriage work.

She watched him, her eyes willing him to come back to her. After listening in silence he gave a brief response in Spanish and replaced the receiver. Turning, he hitched his shirt from the waistband of his trousers, his dark features as rigid as stone, his eyes slightly hooded, impaling her as he let the shirt drop to the floor.

Her heart leapt.

Whatever the call had been about, it hadn't spoiled things. He was coming back to her. He was! Smiling softly, her heart in her eyes, she held out loving arms to him as he reached for the buckle of his belt.

'Teresa tells me my mother has just arrived. She is to lunch with us. Go down to her while I shower and change,' he instructed flatly. 'Tell her I will be ten minutes, no more.'

Her heart sank.

Doña Elvira couldn't have arrived at a worse moment, Cassie thought wretchedly as she watched him turn and walk to the bathroom. Naked now, the lines of his body long and fluid. Perfect. There was a lump in her throat. No word of regret, no soft apology. Nothing. Just a flatly delivered instruction, a long level look that withered her soul.

Was that his way of showing her that he was a mere man after all, pushed by his hormones into accepting what had been so flagrantly offered—despite his reservations?

No. She wouldn't let herself believe that.

There was more than mere lust between them; she knew there was. Briskly, hanging on to that thought, she refastened the lacy bra and swung off the rumpled bed. Their five-week-long idyll told her there was more, much more. Hadn't she got to know the more relaxed side of the man she'd married—the side that was funny, deeply charming, sexy yet tender, sometimes impossibly arrogant but always endlessly endearing?

He was suffering from the effects of plain, old-fashioned sexual frustration. Just as she was. It was perfectly simple, she told herself firmly.

The filmy, flirty, ultra-feminine dress wasn't something she would have normally chosen to wear for lunch with her starchy, ultra-conservative mother-in-law, she thought light-headedly as she slipped it over her head and pulled up the fine side zipper. But these days she dressed to please Roman—she didn't stick to things she hoped her in-laws would deem suitable.

And because she knew her husband's eyes would openly admire the way the narrow seam at the top of the bodice left her lightly tanned arms and most of her shoulders bare, the neckline dipping into a tantalising V, the soft gauzy fabric moulding her breasts and nipping in at her waist to fall with a floaty fullness to just below her knees, the dress pleased her, too.

As usual, Doña Elvira was dressed in black, relieved slightly by just a touch of white silk at her throat. Cassie found her in the small *sala*, where Teresa had set the circular table with the very best china, glass and heavy antique silver.

Meeting the steady, cool assessment of a pair of dark eyes, Cassie gave a small smile and said, 'How nice to see you,' and knew she didn't mean it at all. She hoped this was to be a flying visit only, but she couldn't ask and appear impossibly rude.

'Roman apologises,' Cassie added lightly. 'He's only just back from some business or other in Seville. He'll be a few more minutes and then Teresa will give us lunch.'

'Sanlucar suits you,' the older woman announced from the seat in the window that overlooked the sun-baked terrace, the great Guadalquivir river and the vast Coto Doñana nature reserve. 'I find you—' a pale, long-fingered hand moved questingly '—much improved.'

Coming from one of her severest critics, Cassie

had to take that as a compliment. She spread her hands, 'I find the town, this house, quite beautiful. Who could not be happy here?'

'You were not. Before.'

The words dropped like heavy stones into a deep, dark pool and Cassie knew why the older woman had come here. Curiosity. Uneasy suspicions. She wanted to judge for herself whether the supposed reconciliation was real or just a blind to stop her and her sisters pressing Roman to go ahead with the divorce and marry someone they found acceptable—with Delfina being the obvious and prime candidate.

What would be the other woman's reaction if Cassie told her she was already expecting her son's child?

Suddenly, a wave of compassionate understanding engulfed her. Already she felt fiercely protective of the tiny new life she was carrying inside her. Of course Doña Elvira wanted the best for her son. What mother wouldn't? And three years ago Cassie hadn't been the best.

But she had changed, become more self-confident, able to physically express her love for her husband. This time, if Roman wanted it, the marriage would work.

So she said, gently reassuring, 'No, back then there were problems, mainly of my own making.'

'And they've been resolved?' The tone, as always, was carefully polite, but the cool dark eyes had narrowed watchfully. 'I want only happiness for my son, you understand?'

'I believe so. I believe I could make him happy,' Cassie said, with a sudden and unwelcome hollow feeling inside her.

Some problems had been swept away but others had crowded in to take their place. But it was up to her to resolve that, wasn't it?

She forced herself into a more optimistic frame of mind but couldn't stop her nerves from jangling when Roman said from behind her, 'So what brings you here, *Madre*? So far as I know, you haven't set foot inside this house for fifteen years. Has Cassandra given you something to drink? No? Then let me repair the omission.'

Cool, urbane, totally controlled—who would have thought that ten minutes ago he had succumbed to the wild call of the flesh, against all his obvious mental reservations, had been on the point of making wild, passionate love to her? Cassie thought as she sank on to the padded seat in the deep window embrasure.

Watching him as he poured pale Manzanilla into three tulip glasses, her heart twisted over with regret. Wearing white—beautifully tailored narrow trousers and a silk shirt that fell in long graceful folds from his impressive shoulders—he looked as gorgeous and as remote as a man could get.

Why hadn't she said those things she'd been mentally rehearsing over the last two days the moment he'd walked into the bedroom they shared—instead of flinging herself at him like the sex-mad creature he believed her to have become?

Because she loved him so much, had missed him so badly, she answered herself as he handed her a glass, looking carefully at some point over her left shoulder yet somehow avoiding any contact of their fingers. Her instincts had taken over and her instincts had been wrong. Far better that their short time alone had been occupied in putting him straight.

But she hadn't known that her mother-in-law was about to descend on them, and that lady was saying, her cool features warm now as she spoke to her son, 'True, I haven't been here since your father died. I prefer to keep my memories intact. Remember the summers we spent here—you, your father and I? The horse races on the river beach you both took part in? With me shouting your names and urging you on as loudly as any farmhand? The picnics, the long treks through the Coto Doñana? How happy we were in those days! After he died it could never be the same.'

Her smile faded. She took a sip of her Manzanilla and set the glass down on the small table at her side. 'Perhaps when you give me grandchildren I will be able to spend more happy summers here.'

Here we go again, Cassie thought as she surreptitiously emptied her own drink into the nearest pot plant. Emotional blackmail. She wasn't the only one who'd been subjected to it. Roman obviously had, ever since he'd reached marriageable age.

Thankfully, Teresa arrived, moving deftly around despite her bulk, laying dishes on the table. Doña Elvira said less mournfully, 'I am visiting the house in Jerez now that the decorators have finished. I want to make sure all is exactly as it should be. Tomás is driving me; Teresa is looking after him. I thought I would make this diversion to bring you the news before Tomás and I retrace ourselves to Jerez.'

She stood up, leading the way to the table, and Roman, an indulgent smile on his face for the difficulties his mother sometimes had with the English language, asked, 'And that is?'

Cassie followed, hoping her mother-in-law's news didn't involve Roy and some further misdeed; she felt more miserable by the minute, because Roman had barely looked at her since he'd entered the room—and when he had his expression had been cold.

'I hope it won't come as too much of a shock,' Doña Elvira said as she helped herself generously to swordfish with a luscious prawn and clam sauce, adding a portion of Teresa's roast red pepper and tomato salad. 'I know how close the two of you are—were—and I didn't want you to hear of it through the newspapers. Delfina is engaged to be married.'

'Now why should that shock me?' He spoke softly, as if he were humouring a child. But Cassie had seen the flicker of relief cross his face.

His ploy had paid off. Darling Delfina was off his back. But what had started off as a tactical manoeuvre, with her playing the part of a returning loving wife in exchange for Roy's freedom from prosecution, had turned into something wonderful. A marriage that could truly work. Surely to God it had?

Her hands were knotted together in her lap, her knuckles white. She barely heard Doña Elvira's, 'Delfina's such a lovely girl. Your aunts and I, we always hoped—'

'I know what you hoped,' Roman cut in sardonically, helping himself to a chunk of crusty bread to mop up the delicious sauce. 'And I think you know I won't tolerate any more meddling. Don't even think about dredging up some other suitable, shallow creature to dangle in front of my nose now Delfina's out of the frame. I forbid it.'

Cassie's stomach twisted alarmingly. Her throat went tight. Why didn't he remind his mother that he already had a wife? Sitting right here! Why were they both ignoring her? Doña Elvira quite naturally, probably because she believed Cassie wasn't worth noticing, and Roman studiedly, as if he didn't want to be reminded that she existed.

Well, she *did* exist—she *would* be noticed! She unstuck her tongue from the roof of her mouth and asked firmly, 'So, who is the lucky man?'

A heartbeat of silence, then Doña Elvira said lightly, 'You wouldn't know him.' She turned to her son. 'Rodrigo Talavera. They are to be married in Brazil, where most of his family is. They leave in a few days; her mother goes with her, naturally.'

'He's old enough to be her father.'

Roman looked faintly amused, the smile that played around the corner of his mouth deepening as his mother defended, 'But wealthy. He will dote on her and spoil her thoroughly. She will be happy. And you, Cassandra, you are not eating?'

Suddenly, the attention was on Cassie. She felt her face go hot.

'I'm not really hungry,' she said truthfully. How could she eat a thing when her stomach was tied in squirming knots? She wanted the meal over and done with, her mother-in-law out of the way so that she could talk to Roman, really talk to him, tell him what was in her heart and discover what was in his.

'Is it Spain that robs you of your appetite? It is obvious that you ate well when you were in your own country.' Dark eyes pointedly raked the fullness of the breasts emphasised by the clinging bodice, the smoothly rounded arms. 'You were happier back in your own country, I think?'

The implication being she should go right back there, Cassie thought on a flash of temper. She fingered the stem of her water glass, looking at Roman from beneath her lashes, and said with a trace of defiance, 'I've been wonderfully happy here and, yes, if the record needs straightening, I was happy back in England, too.'

She wasn't going to pull any punches. Roman, in particular, needed to know what had happened to her. He hadn't really asked, and she'd been too bound up in the enchantment of getting to know him physically, in the strong rebirth of her love for him, to tell him.

Aware of his brooding attention, she said, 'At the risk of sounding fanciful, I discovered who I was

during my year away. I'd never had to be responsible
for myself; all decisions had been made for me—by
my father, my husband, my in-laws.'

She heard Doña Elvira's intake of breath and ignored it. 'For the first time in my life I was responsible for myself. It was scary at first, but exhilarating.
I headed for my home town because I knew it, had
friends there.' She met Roman's thoughtful eyes
head-on. 'I found a cheap bed-sit, walked into a wai-
tressing job, enrolled in a couple of evening
classes—upholstery and furniture restoration—and
made a few new friends. I was in charge of my own
life, my own well-being and making a reasonable fist
of it.

'Then, six weeks or so later, Cindy offered me a
job helping her run the boutique. One of the perks
was the rent-free flat above it. I took it—of course I
did. It was a far better proposition than what I was
doing, where I was living.' She took a breath.

'But most important of all, it was *my* decision.
Nobody was telling me what to do and how to do it.
Nobody was making me feel inferior and pretty damn
useless. And at last I had a home I could call my
own. Could decorate it and furnish it just as I wanted
to—mainly cheap second-hand stuff—and that's
where the evening classes came in useful.'

No need to say that Guy had helped her trawl the
auction rooms, had wielded a paintbrush pretty nif-
tily. No need to put suspicions in Roman's mind that
had no right to be there.

No need to mention how very much she'd missed

her arrogant Spanish husband, or how hard she'd tried not to, how hard she'd tried to put the past behind her. Not now, not while she could feel Doña Elvira's eyes on her, absorbing every word she said. Later, when they were alone, she would tell him that missing him had been the hardest part of all.

'So.' She tugged in a breath. 'In a nutshell, I finally grew up. Learned to stand on my own two feet, got some self-respect. Now—' she glanced around the table. '—we appear to have finished. Shall I ask Teresa for coffee?' She looked at her mother-in-law and caught the slightly astonished gleam of admiration in the older woman's eyes as she proffered, 'Or shall I ask her to tell Tomás to bring the car round? You must be eager to settle into the newly decorated house. If you're staying there for more than a day or two, maybe Roman and I will descend on you for a tour of inspection.'

Half an hour later, after seeing Doña Elvira off—very upright and dignified in the back of the ancient Daimler that was kept for ferrying his elderly relatives around—Roman said, 'Among other things, you've learned how to handle her.'

It was the 'other things' that had to be sorted out, Cassie thought, following him back inside into the relatively cool, echoing dimness of the massive hall.

Would he believe her when she insisted she hadn't spent that year away sleeping around, learning by experience? He hadn't so far, but that didn't mean she wasn't going to try again.

Would he truly understand that, apart from his monumental Spanish pride being damaged by having a runaway wife, that year had been necessary? He'd said she'd needed to grow up, but more than that, she had needed to find out who she was, what she was capable of—had needed to find the self-respect that had been missing for most of her life.

Roman looked so sombre. She had her misgivings, and they deepened when he turned to face her, his features shadowed and stark in the cool dim light.

'I want you to know that I made a bad mistake when I blackmailed you into staying with me, sleeping with me. I've thought hard about this over the past few days. What I did was unworthy, dishonourable. Unforgivable.' He pushed his hands into his trouser pockets, his mouth a straight hard line, his eyes dark and unreadable.

A current of fear arced through her. What was going on here? Was this some kind of coded message? Would she ever be able to breach those vast, remote defences of his? Could her words alone touch him? He had retreated to a place where she couldn't reach him, just as he had done when he'd decided she was frigid and had ceased to bother with her.

At least she could try! 'You don't have to apologise for anything,' she said quickly.

'I'm not. Haven't I already said that what I did was unforgivable? So,' he went on in a flat monotone, 'you are free to go now. I release you from our bargain. And before you start worrying about that brother of yours—who should be old enough to look after himself—if he keeps his nose clean, works hard, he can enjoy a good position on the *finca*.'

Dismissed. Just like that! These few weeks had meant nothing to him. A woman to sleep with, that was all she'd been to him, and now she'd served her purpose she could go.

Anger sparked in her eyes. 'Let me get this straight—Delfina's safely engaged and due to leave the country in a day or two, and,' she added for good measure, 'you've satisfied your curiosity about my present attitude to sex, so I can leave!'

She hadn't known she could feel this betrayed, so surplus to requirements. Or so blisteringly angry! At least anger was keeping the hurt away—for the moment.

He seemed to be having a problem with her anger, judging by the frowning bar of his brows. And then he tilted his head just slightly. 'If that's how you want to see it. I am merely explaining you are free to go.'

Or stay? But he hadn't mentioned anything about her staying. And she could tell by the closed-in look on his face that her presence was suddenly distasteful to him. But she'd give him one last chance; she owed that to herself and to their unborn child.

'What about the divorce?' she asked, and wished she hadn't sounded quite so humble. She prayed he'd say he didn't want that to happen, prayed so hard her heart hurt.

'If that's what you want,' Roman conceded slowly. His minimal shrug looked decidedly dismissive. 'But in the meantime I'll make you a generous allowance. I know, because you've told me—' his mouth curved bitterly, '—that you're quite capable of looking after yourself, but the job and the flat you had have gone. For that I take full responsibility—and I don't like the idea of you having to wait on tables, or serve behind some seedy bar because you're unqualified for anything better, living on a low wage in some squalid room.'

It was like a slap in the face. A hard slap. Holding herself together was going to be tough. She lifted her chin and said staunchly, 'Then I'll pack. I'll stay overnight in Seville and catch the first available flight back to England.'

She headed for the stairs, but his harsh voice halted her. 'Tell me when you're ready and I'll drive you.'

She didn't turn. She couldn't. Why let him see the tears that were now flowing unstoppably? She swallowed hard. 'Thanks but I'd much prefer Manuel's company. Perhaps you could tell him I'll be ready to leave in twenty minutes.'

CHAPTER ELEVEN

ROMAN dismounted and handed the reins of his sweat-lathered horse to the groom who came hurrying from the stable block to meet him. Beneath the straight brim of his black, dust-covered Cordoban hat his features were scored with harsh lines.

The sun was setting, casting long shadows over the sweeping upland valley; a pair of eagles planed overhead in a cloudless sky that was deepening to amethyst.

His boots rang on the cobbles of the yard as he strode towards the main house, slapping the dust from the sleeves of his heavy-duty canvas jacket.

Nothing had worked during the month since Cassie had left. Not a damn thing. Not the long hours of unremitting physical hard work here on the estate, the endless cold showers, stern and lengthy lectures to himself on the advisability of cutting his losses, getting on with his life, etc, etc.

Something had died inside him when she'd walked out of their marriage for the second time. Only his ingrained pride had stopped him from going after her, up the sweeping staircase he never wanted to have to see again in the whole of his life, begging her to forgive him, pleading with her to stay.

The first time she'd left him had been hard. This time it was a whole lot tougher.

He'd given her the opportunity to leave, and against all his hopes she'd taken it. But what else, with honour, could he have done? To have put pressure on her to stay with him would have been unthinkable, given what he'd already done to her.

Initially, the idea of forcing her to stay with him had seemed logical. It would have given them the chance to get to know each other all over again, allow him to prove that he could be good husband material. Not the remote figure he'd turned into during the first two years of their marriage, too insensitive, or too damn proud to ask why she flinched and looked at him with frightened eyes whenever he came near her.

But later the idea of blackmail had left a sour taste in his mouth. He'd come to despise himself for using her natural concern for her brother against her. And, yes, if he was honest with himself, jealousy had come into it. Where and how had she learned to be so sexually responsive? And who with?

Now that side of it didn't seem to matter. Provided it was in the past.

As usual, Asunción had left a cold supper on a tray in his study. Food had been the last thing on his mind these past weeks.

And, thankfully, the aunts had joined his mother in Jerez for the Sherry Harvest that had been celebrated earlier this month. He could do without the presence of chattering females and he guessed the

icy tongue-lashing he'd doled out on the subject of
their less than helpful treatment of Cass in the past
had sent them scuttling for cover, staying at the
house in Jerez for much longer than usual, hoping
that time would improve his temper.

Time wouldn't alter a thing; he knew that. Only
his wife's love could make him feel whole again.

Roy, too, had moved out to one of the self-
contained *cabañas* on the estate, so that meant he
was alone here and no one but himself had to suffer
from his perpetual black mood.

If it weren't for his pride he might not have been
alone. He might have had Cass. His wife. His adored
wife. But he hadn't told her how beloved she was.
He ground his teeth together, raging against himself.
He'd been on the brink of it, willing himself to swallow his pride, tell her how he felt and put his future
happiness in her hands—when two things had happened.

A sudden brain-boiling hatred for the man—or
men—who had taught Cassie to enjoy sex, and an
equally explosive reaction to the way he'd blackmailed her into agreeing to live with him.

Ignoring his supper, as he did more often than not,
he tossed his hat onto a chair and reached for the
phone.

Stiff-necked, arrogant pride.

It didn't warm his bed or fill his heart with joy.
One thing was for sure: he had to see her one more
time, swallow that wretched pride of his—go down
on his knees if necessary and humbly ask if she

would forget the idea of a divorce and spend the rest of her life with him. And if she would, he'd make sure she never regretted a single moment of their time together.

And if she didn't—well, he didn't want to think about that. But he'd be no worse off than he was now. What did loss of pride matter?

His face grimly determined, he punched in the numbers for Air Iberia.

Cassie stepped out of the bath and smothered her glowing body in the swamping towelling robe Guy had loaned her and felt marginally better.

The weather on this first day of October had turned wet and decidedly chilly, an unpleasant and unseasonal foretaste of winter. She'd got soaked to the skin as she'd walked back to the ground-floor flat from the antiquarian bookshop where she'd found part-time, temporary work.

Four days a week, from ten in the morning until four in the afternoon, Robert Greaves—the owner—had told her. The job would end in November, when his partner returned from visiting relatives in New Zealand.

It wasn't much but it was better than nothing and at least the pay packet meant she didn't have to dip into her savings account. Soon she would have to start looking for something else.

A sudden mental image of the cheque Roman had sent through Cindy flashed into her consciousness.

She blinked it rapidly away as she dragged a comb through her tangled wet hair.

As an allowance it had been more than generous. She wouldn't have had to find work to keep her and the baby growing inside her. But she hadn't even been tempted. She wanted nothing from him. He'd virtually accused her of marrying him in the first place for what she could get out of him, deliberately causing the breakdown of their relationship so that on their divorce she could take him to the cleaners.

Well, he could stuff his wretched money! She could manage without it!

'Send it straight back to him,' she'd instructed Cindy tersely, tearing the cheque to tiny pieces.

'Are you mad?' Cindy's blue eyes had gone wide. 'I don't know what went wrong this time—I've lost patience with the pair of you—but why scratch around for a living when Roman can afford to keep you in comfort?'

'Because I don't want his hand-outs.' She wanted his love, and because she knew she couldn't have it she was damned if she'd settle for anything less. Besides, regular contact, even if it was only through a monthly allowance cheque, would remind her of him, hamper her resolve to forget he'd ever existed.

'Then *you* return it,' Cindy had ordered, refusing to take the confetti-like scraps of paper. 'You do know his address! Besides, this not speaking to each other is childish. You could at least talk things over like rational human beings. Heaven knows, he can afford to keep you until you get back on your feet. Absolutely childish!' she'd repeated vehemently.

Perhaps. But the pain of what he had done to Cassie, using her body until he got bored then giving her her marching orders, was entirely adult and ferocious.

'You haven't told him where I am?' Cassie had asked, her eyes narrowing suspiciously.

'Nope. He didn't ask. When he phoned he just said he'd be sending a cheque once a month and would I see you got it.'

Yet another savage stab of pain. He wasn't interested in her whereabouts, what she was doing. For all he knew or cared, she could have emigrated to Australia!

Though why that should hurt when she'd already decided that she had no interest in him either, she couldn't fathom. She'd drawn a decisive line beneath her ill-fated marriage to Roman Fernandez—hadn't she?

Cassie slammed the door firmly on memories that had anything at all to do with Roman—something, she reflected uneasily, she was having to do several times a day. She put the hairbrush down on the dressing table and walked out of the tiny spare bedroom, tightening the belt of her robe around her waist.

It was almost five o'clock and Guy would be home in an hour, from the high street travel agency he managed, and since making use of his spare room she'd insisted on cooking supper. It was the least she could do.

She would put the remains of yesterday's casserole in the oven and then throw on a pair of jeans and a warm sweater. Then, while the casserole was heating through, she'd prepare a salad to go with it and cut up the crusty loaf she'd bought on her way home.

She was straightening up after sliding the heavy cast-iron pot into the oven when she caught the sound of a key in the door.

'You're back early,' she said, her breath snagging at the rapt expression in Guy's warm hazel eyes as he looked at her from the open kitchen doorway. She knew her face had to be flushed from the blast of heat she'd received from the oven, all mixed up with a tide of uneasy embarrassment. She'd meant to be dressed before he got back.

The robe was smothering enough in all conscience, but the implication was that she was naked beneath it, and the way Guy was looking at her told her he was fully aware of that fact.

The situation here was growing more awkward by the day.

Thankfully, it would soon be over.

'Yes. I decided to shut up shop early. There's no business around. Time of year, I guess. Plus, people appear to be organising their own holidays on the internet.'

Guy closed the door behind him, walking further into the room. The kitchen was doll's-house size and Cassie was beginning to feel claustrophobic. Cindy had told her how her brother felt about her, and Roman had suspected it. She should never have al-

lowed herself to be pressured into staying here. He
was a dear friend and hurting him was the last thing
she wanted to do.

'I thought we might eat out this evening,' Guy
said, removing his tie, his eyes never leaving her
face. 'There's something I want to say to you.'

'Then say it here,' she responded lightly.

But her throat tightened miserably. She hoped it
wasn't what she thought it was. Ever since he'd
found out about her pregnancy—she hadn't been able
to keep it from him; her regular bouts of morning
sickness would have alerted a fool—he had been different. More serious, more watchful—possessive,
even.

'Bastard!' he'd said when she'd reluctantly admitted his suspicions were right, pressing him to promise to keep the knowledge to himself, at least until
she'd sorted herself out. Because, much as she loved
her friend, she couldn't absolutely trust Cindy not to
pass the news on to Roman. 'If I could get my hands
on him I'd throttle him for what he's done to you!'

She reached a head of lettuce from the fridge.
'Supper's already on the way. I've been soaked
through once, and so, by the looks of it, have you. I
don't fancy a repeat performance. Why don't you
change while I finish off? And, by the way—' she
reached for a knife and began to shred the lettuce
into a colander '—I'll be moving out at the end of
the week. I found a bed-sit in Church Street today.'

She turned on the tap—anything to break the sudden stinging silence. Then he said, 'There's no need for that. You know there isn't.'

'There's every need,' she responded seriously. 'I want to be independent. It was good of you to take me in—'

'Good!' His mouth twisted on the interruption. 'Don't go all mealy-mouthed on me! Cin and I had to practically twist your arm before you'd take up my offer. Mum and Dad were in the process of selling up and retiring to the Lakes and Cin had just moved in with her boyfriend. Staying here was the last and least-favoured option, so don't try to pretend it wasn't,' he challenged bitterly.

The only other option being a bed and breakfast place, as they'd both been at pains to point out. For the first few days back in the small Shropshire market town where she'd lived for most of her life she'd stayed in a run-down boarding house on the outskirts and had seen what a drain it could make on her modest savings.

Finding a job had been her first priority, and she'd only reluctantly agreed to accept Guy's offer of a roof over her head until she could find a place of her own.

What could she say? In the past she'd been thankful for his friendship, his help, looking on him as a brother—one more reliable than the one she had! It was only since learning how he really felt about her that she'd wanted as little to do with him as possible.

She had first-hand knowledge of how it felt to love

and not be loved in return. She didn't want to make him hurt any more than he already was.

She gave him what she hoped was a pacifying smile and turned back to the sink. 'I have been grateful, truly. But it's time to move on. It never was a permanent arrangement; you know that. Besides— think about it—you don't want a divorcee plus child cluttering up your space. It would seriously cramp your style. From what I've heard—' she injected a note of wry humour to let him know she wasn't being judgemental or the least bit envious, was merely stating a fact '—you've accumulated a fair few notches on your bedpost in the past.'

She heard Guy approach. Felt his hand on her shoulder, tightening just briefly, heard the complacency in his voice as he said, 'If that's all that's bothering you, we don't have a problem. We'll sort this out over supper.'

He walked out of the room and she knew she'd blown it. He had misread her—believed she'd been fishing for reassurance about her place in his life, his intentions.

Roman paid off the taxi as the clock on the church tower struck five and turned up the collar of his leather jacket against the cold driving rain. The brightly lit windows of the boutique reflected splashes of orange and gold on the wet pavements.

The sign on the glass door said 'closed', but he could see Cindy's blonde head bent over some paperwork on the desk at the back of the bright little shop.

His stride was as confident as ever, his knuckle-rap on the glass of the door imperious. But inside his heart he was terrified.

He had little doubt that he could persuade his distant cousin to tell him how to find his runaway wife. But would Cassie agree to come back to him? Could she ever learn to love him again? Once, she had loved him—she'd told him as much. But had the precious magic gone for ever?

Cindy's pretty face was wreathed in smiles as she unlocked the door and held it open. 'You've come for Cass,' she stated. 'About time, too.'

He followed her in, the warm, cheerful atmosphere barely impinging, and Cindy said, 'Come through to the back before you drip all over those silk blouses.'

Carefully negotiating the racks of colourful garments, he sank into a chair opposite the one she'd been using, stuffing his hands into the pockets of his black denims, his long legs outstretched and his booted feet crossed at the ankles.

'I take it she hasn't sworn you to secrecy on the subject of her whereabouts?' he divined from her opening remarks.

'Of course she has!' Cindy answered blithely, turning to the small counter behind her to switch on an electric kettle. 'But, like the first time she did a runner, I'm prepared to break my word for the good of all concerned. One thing I do promise, though, I'll never tell her that I reported regularly to you, that you persuaded me to give her a job here when Kelly left to have her baby, or that you paid the rent on the flat that was supposed to be one of the perks.'

She spooned coffee granules into two heavy earthenware mugs. 'Cass grew wonderfully in self-confidence during that year. It would knock her back if she knew you'd been keeping a watching brief. She's such an innocent in a lot of ways. She never questioned why her job with me was so well paid—thanks to your top-up cheques. I don't think she'd be all that happy to know you've been there behind the scenes, helping her. I thought I should warn you against letting that cat out of the bag!'

'Thanks.' He managed a smile but his face felt stiff with tension. Cindy had a point. It had been a joy to see Cassie's new aura of self-assurance, to see her reach her full potential as a woman.

When she'd left him that first time he'd been frantic, stunned by the realisation of how much she meant to him. Despite the seeming failure of their marriage, the bitter knowledge that he hadn't done enough to try and make it work had made him hate himself.

His first instinct had been to follow her, do something positive about the situation. Sober reflection had stopped him. Only then had he been able to see clearly. All her life she'd been dominated, one way or another. She'd never had the chance to find out who she really was or what she was capable of. Time on her own, without a father, a husband or a clutch of in-laws to tell her what to do and how to do it, would only help her.

With him keeping an eye on her through Cindy, giving an unseen helping hand. And one day, when the time was right, when he judged she would believe herself to be his equal, he would ask her to come back to him.

But fate, in the shape of her brother's criminal activities, had intervened. And he'd made an unholy mess of it.

One day, though, when their marriage was firm, her love for him as strong and enduring as his was for her, then he would tell her how carefully he'd watched over her well-being. There were to be no secrets between them.

'Drink that. You look as if you need it.' Cindy put a mug of steaming coffee in front of him, breaking into his teeming thoughts. 'You look as if you haven't eaten or slept for weeks.'

It was too near the truth to bother arguing with. He took a gulp of the scalding brew, watching intently as she found a piece of paper, her pen flying as she scrawled an address.

'I don't know what went wrong; she didn't tell me. I was really sure the two of you would make a go of it this time, but when she arrived back here she looked as if her world had fallen apart.'

'My fault,' he admitted tightly, his heart beating with sudden hope. If he'd been no more than a stud to her, a way of satisfying her new-found sexuality while she'd been blackmailed into staying with him;

if she'd been happy to see the back of him—as her headlong flight had suggested—then she wouldn't have appeared to be so shattered, would she?

Cindy pushed the scrap of paper over the desk, her eyes narrowing as she debated the wisdom of telling him or not that his wife was temporarily staying with her brother.

Not, she decided. Roman's pride was legendary. He might turn round and go straight back to Spain if he knew Cassie was sharing a roof with another man.

On the other hand, Roman knew that the three of them had been close friends for practically the whole of their lives. He didn't know Guy was in love with Cass. And Cass wasn't interested; she was still in love with her husband.

Cindy sighed. They would have to sort it out for themselves. By telling him where to find Cass she'd done more than her fair share of meddling. 'It's a ten-minute walk, if that,' she told him. 'But I could call a cab; it's still pouring down outside.'

'I'll walk, if you'll give me directions.' He stood up, impatient to be gone. It would probably take a cab more than ten minutes to turn up here and a drop of rain wouldn't hurt him.

At the door, after giving him the simple directions, Cindy said, almost diffidently, 'I don't know what your plans are, and I know you're great at granting favours but lousy at taking them, but you can stay with us tonight. Fraser and I only have the one bed at the moment, but you could kip on the sofa. Cass has our number—call. One of us can pick you up.'

'So you see this as something of a wild-goose chase?' The forced lightness of his tone hid the sudden swamping ache that tightened his heart. 'What's to say I won't be spending the night, the rest of my life, with Cass?'

The hope was so great it tore at him savagely. But if it didn't turn out that way—his body went cold, his heart contracting beneath a layer of ice—then company would be the last thing he wanted. He would rather walk the streets, or find an all-night cab company and get himself straight back to the airport.

He gave Cindy a bleak smile and strode out into the rain.

Her hands unsteady, Cassie hastily chopped red peppers, sweet onions and celery and dumped them into the bowl of lettuce. She'd make the dressing later.

She had to get dressed before Guy had finished getting showered and changed. Suitably armoured against the hungry look she'd seen in his eyes, she'd be more able to explain that he'd made the wrong assumptions, that she would never see him as anything other than a friend.

Explain, perhaps, that she still loved Roman and probably always would, despite what had happened. Not that Guy had any idea, of course. He only knew what she'd told him and Cindy—that the reconciliation hadn't worked out. That didn't stop him being anti-Roman. Guy blamed him for everything bad that had happened in her life.

And maybe he was right.

But there were good things, too, memories she would always treasure. Memories of a time when she'd believed that their lives would run together, always. Those lazy, languid weeks in Sanlucar. The sun and the teasing wind from the Atlantic. Wandering through the old town together, hand in hand, sipping *café solos* at their favourite café, where the taped voices of *cante jondo* singers came from the dim interior and a fragrant orange tree cast a welcome shade over their chosen table. And the nights, the long, sultry nights of loving…

The knife she'd been holding slipped from her nerveless fingers, skittering over the tiled floor. Blinking, biting her lip as she came back to stark reality, she muttered under her breath and went down on her knees to fish it out from under the fridge.

And heard the kitchen door open.

Damn!

She'd been day-dreaming, masochistically indulging in memories that only served to heighten her pain, when she should have been starching herself up, dressing in sexless old jeans and a baggy sweater, scraping back her hair.

Now she would really have to scuttle if Guy weren't to get the wrong ideas about her state of undress.

Giving up on the knife that seemed to have got well and truly wedged, she peered through the nearly-dry mane of her hair, her startled eyes fastening on a pair of boots, travelling slowly up long, lithely muscled legs encased in narrow black denim, a black leather jacket spangled with raindrops.

Roman!

His black hair was plastered to his skull and there were lines of strain etched deeply at the sides of his mouth, but his eyes glowed with something that made her breath catch in her throat, her heartbeats race, sending her giddy.

'The door was on the latch. I walked straight in.' His voice was like velvet, the voice of the lover who had haunted her dreams. 'You should be more security-conscious, Cass. I worry about you.' A slow, almost tentative smile curved his mouth. 'At least something smells good. You are not neglecting yourself, as I feared.'

The casserole! she thought manically, trying to hold on to the mundane and normal to counteract the shock of his sudden appearance, the crazy hopes that against all common sense were clamouring for recognition in her painfully agitated brain.

It was an effort to scramble to her feet, an effort to make her voice work. 'Why are you here?' It was scarcely more than a whisper. She couldn't tear her eyes from his face. So dear to her, so loved. Yet strangely older, with deeper hollows beneath his slashing cheekbones. Compassion stirred strongly, making her ache. Had he, too, suffered, just as she had?

His slightly hooded eyes swept her, a line of quick

colour touching his skin, and Cassie, shell-shocked, knew why when she glanced down and saw how during her undignified knife-hunt the edges of her borrowed robe had come apart, revealing the heavy globes of her breasts, or most of them, the line of her still-flat tummy and the tangle of springy hair at the apex of her thighs.

Swallowing convulsively, she snatched at the edges, wrapping them tightly around her, and he said thickly, moving closer, 'Don't hide your body from me. You are so beautiful you make my heart ache, *querida*. I have come for you, if you will have me. Will you, my Cassie?'

With tears in her eyes, dazed wonder numbing her mind, her body suddenly shaking, Cassie could only struggle to get control of her vocal cords, tell him yes, and yes again, to be with him was what she had always wanted.

A sound emerged, but thickly, making no sense. Her hands flew to her face as shattering emotions racked her body. She made her feet move somehow towards him, to reply to his question with physical contact, since she seemed incapable of doing it verbally—her body against his, her arms around him, her mouth finding his, giving him his answer.

'Stop hounding her, dammit!' Guy's voice was thin and high, ragged with temper. 'Haven't you done enough damage?'

In the doorway his face was red. He was wearing a thin silky robe that did little to disguise the fact that he wore nothing under it.

The silence following his outburst was still and sharp. Cassie didn't know whether to giggle hysterically or to burst into tears.

Roman turned cold eyes on his distant cousin, his patrician nostrils pinched with arctic displeasure.

'And don't look at me like that,' Guy blustered. 'This is my home, and I'm telling you we don't want you in it. If you need to contact Cassie, do it through your solicitor.'

Cassie's eyes went wide. Guy's face was purple now. She was afraid he'd have a stroke! 'Guy,' she commanded, as firmly as she could under these surreal circumstances, 'don't I have a say here?'

'No!' His voice rose a full octave. 'I'm handling this. And I'll tell you something for nothing, Fernandez. I'm looking after Cass, I'm marrying her and taking care of the baby—'

A single fiery Spanish expletive cut him off in full flow. Tormented charcoal eyes flicked briefly in Cassie's direction. And then, with Guy stepping smartly aside, Roman strode through the doorway, disappearing into the dark wet night.

CHAPTER TWELVE

'THIS is a total dump!' Cindy censured, parking herself on the only armchair the dingy room boasted. The best that could be said of it was that it had broken springs and stained upholstery. 'Guy was in a right state when he phoned this morning and told me you'd moved out, and where you'd gone. I came as soon as I shut up shop. Where's Roman?' she demanded. 'And what the hell do you think you're doing in this grot-hole? Honestly, sometimes I think you should be locked up for your own safety!'

Glumly, Cassie had to agree with her friend's scathing assessment of the bed-sit she'd just moved into. But it was cheap and, more importantly, she was no longer sharing with Guy.

Last night he'd gone to bed in a chastened mood after she'd told him he'd ruined everything for her, reminding him that if he'd thought by saying he was planning on marrying her and looking after the baby had been an act of chivalry, he was utterly and hopelessly wrong.

What he'd said, giving Roman the wrong impression of their relationship, had been totally destructive and completely out of order.

She'd spent the night in anguish, stuffing her few

possessions in carrier bags, then pacing the floor as she waited for dawn when she could remove herself; sleep had been out of the question.

Roman had wanted her back, wanted to make their marriage work. Now he believed she'd shacked up with Guy, leapt straight into bed with him and had conceived his child. What other interpretation could he have put on what Guy had said? No wonder he'd walked straight out. He would think she was a slut and would have washed his hands of her!

'So,' Cindy prompted sharply, 'what happened? Roman had come for you; I know that because I gave him Guy's address. Don't tell me you sent him packing?'

Still in shock over what had happened the previous evening, and cursing the weak tears that flooded her eyes, Cassie muttered dully, 'It's a long story.' She really didn't want to talk about it. It was too close, too painful. But she knew she would have to. Cindy wouldn't leave until she did.

Buying herself a few extra moments, she offered tiredly, 'Why don't I make us some coffee?'

There was a sink and a gas ring in one corner, divided from the rest of the room by a shabby brown curtain. She'd shopped for a few basics on her way back from the bookshop but hadn't been motivated enough to unpack them.

Now she hunted through the carrier for the jar of granules, and when the brew was made and she couldn't delay any longer she perched on the edge of the single bed and haltingly told her friend everything.

'Hell's teeth!' Cindy exploded, putting her empty mug down on the floor. 'How could my stupid brother have done that? I honestly thought it would be all right—he kept his feelings to himself, was the perfect gentleman, in fact, when you came back that first time.'

She moved her hands expressively, her frown ferocious. 'The only time he ever really came clean about what he felt for you, he definitely told me he wouldn't say a word to you, or give you a hint, while you were still legally married to Roman. I really thought it would be the same this time, otherwise—' She shook her head helplessly. 'I'm so sorry, Cass!'

'You're not your brother's keeper,' Cassie said dully. 'It's done now.'

'But not dusted,' Cindy replied decisively. 'When did you find out you were pregnant?'

'Some time towards the end of August, I suppose. Just before everything went wrong.'

'So why didn't you tell Roman then? Surely he'd have been delighted—why keep it a secret?'

'Because.'

Cassie sucked in a long breath. Her whole body was shaking with inner tension. She didn't think she could take much more.

'Because what?'

Another dredging sigh, then Cassie spilled out edgily, 'Because even though we were getting along fine and the sex was great, he hadn't said a word about loving me or wanting me with him permanently. So far as I knew, he still expected me to leave at the end of the three months—he never said a single thing to make me believe anything else. As it happened,' she tacked on stiffly, 'he as good as gave me my marching orders well before then—as soon as he heard Delfina was no longer a problem.'

'All that tells me is that both of you are hopeless when it comes to communication. It doesn't tell me why he doesn't know he's about to be a father,' the other woman pointed out drily.

'If I'd told him about the baby he would have insisted I stay. I do know that much!' Cassie bit down on her trembling lower lip. 'Can't you understand? I needed him to want me for my own sake, not because I was carrying his baby. He wants an heir. And you know him—if I'd refused to stay on permanently because I couldn't bear to stay married to a man who couldn't love me, he would have done everything he could to get custody. I *want* this baby!'

His child.

'It's *his* baby, too,' Cindy pointed out. 'You have to tell him.'

'He thinks it's Guy's.'

'Then you'll have to tell him it isn't, won't you?' Cindy stood up, pointing out firmly, 'You're understandably upset, and in no mood to think straight. But believe me, Roman does love you. Why else would he have asked you to go back to him? But my stupid brother went and put his foot in it. No big deal—just a minor spanner in the works. It's up to you to get everything running smoothly again.'

Cindy had offered to come to Las Colinas Verdes with her for moral support. Now, drawing the hired car up in front of the large stone-built farmhouse at the heart of the sprawling estate, Cassie wished she'd accepted her offer.

It was almost dark. The wind blowing from the distant mountains carried an autumnal chill. She shivered, but the palms of her hands were clammy with sweat.

After Cindy had left her, a couple of evenings ago, she had eventually emerged from her traumatised state and everything had seemed so simple.

Follow Roman back to Spain and tell him the truth.

The baby was his, not Guy's.

Despite the way things had looked, he would believe her—surely he would? After all, he must have missed her, missed the closeness they'd shared, thought things over and regretted having told her to go. He must have done; there could be no other reason for his coming to England, asking her to come back to him.

Simple. The outcome a foregone happy conclusion. She'd felt so sure of herself, and of him, that she'd told her boss at the bookshop that she wouldn't be returning; given up the bed-sit; burned all her bridges.

Now, within moments of coming face to face with

Roman, it didn't seem simple at all. Scary was nearer the mark. What did she know of him? Really know? That he could be tender, caring, a considerate lover, a wildly passionate lover, a wonderful companion—and could change in the blink of an eye into a remote and quelling stranger, keeping his thoughts to himself, his motives an enigma, shutting her out.

She shuddered and forced herself to leave the car, wiping her damp palms down the sides of the cream-coloured linen trousers she wore. It was no use hanging around outside, regretting the impulsive decision that had brought her here. Get it over with. Stop dithering; find some of that self-confidence you were so proud of having achieved, she instructed herself.

Surely it hadn't all gone. Surely she wasn't back right where she'd started at the beginning of their marriage—a timid, tongue-tied little doormat?

However, deciding not to tempt fate, she left her overnight case right where it was on the passenger seat, tucked a few wayward strands of copper-coloured curls behind her ears, resolutely straightened her spine and walked briskly towards the main door.

As always, the heavy, carved door was unlocked. Trying to ignore the shudders of apprehension that were starting up again, playing havoc with her insides, she pushed it open.

What if he threw her straight back out again, refused to even listen to her?

Or what if he did listen, did believe the baby was his, and wanted the baby but not her? He'd already voiced suspicions that she'd been taught by some other man—or men—to be sexually responsive.

Seeing her and Guy together in a virtual state of undress—sharing the same flat only weeks after leaving his bed—would have confirmed everything bad he'd thought about her. Would he fight her through the courts for custody of his child? Would he win?

Either scenario was intolerable, would inflict a wound that would never heal. Trouble was, as Roy had once said, Roman had a mind like a maze. No one ever knew what he was thinking.

Swallowing convulsively, she bit her lip and listened. The main part of the house was silent. The atmosphere empty. No one here. Dragging in a breath, she made for the kitchen regions.

She opened the door to be met by a waft of heat, the aroma of cooking. The sound of rapid Spanish male voices ceased abruptly and Asunción turned from the range, an iron skillet in one hand. Her broad face beamed.

'Señora—you have come. It is good!'

She advanced, edging round the end of the long table where the unmarried estate workers were eating. 'We did not expect, did not know—el patrón he did not say. But I will have Maria make a fire for you. I will make you huevos flamencos—very quick, not much waiting for you.'

'Thanks, Asunción.' Cassie managed a weak smile. 'But I'm not hungry, truly. And please don't go to the trouble of lighting a fire.'

The family was away; it was obvious. And where

was Roman? She'd been so certain he would have come back to his estate in Andalusia when he'd turned on his heel, his head high, his back rigid with that ingrained Spanish pride as he'd stalked out on her.

She'd already glimpsed Roy's bright head among the dark ones around the long table; now he pushed his half-eaten meal away and stood up. There was relief on his face as he walked towards her.

Conversation gradually picked up around the table. Cutlery scraped against plates and someone laughed, the atmosphere going back to normal. Reaching her side, Roy more or less echoed the housekeeper's greeting.

'Sis—thank God you've finally come back!' He gripped her arm, just above her elbow, his fingers urgent through the sleeve of her light linen jacket, marching her back out of the kitchen door, closing it behind them. 'We need to talk.'

Cassie dug her heels in. Much as she loved her brother, she was in no state to listen to his problems, whatever they were. 'Where's Roman?' she asked sharply. 'Do you know?'

'Sanlucar. Look, I'll tell you what I know when we get to my place. We won't be disturbed and there won't be anyone listening at doors. There's enough gossip going the rounds as it is.'

'He is all right, isn't he?' She cast him a worried look. It all sounded ominous.

'Apart from a thunderous black temper, yes. So far as I know.'

Knowing she wouldn't get any more out of him, she gave in and followed as he strode through the stable yard and into a walled quadrangle. Lights glowed from the windows of a dozen stone built *cabañas*, some large, for the married workers and their families, and others smaller, for the bachelors.

'You're not still living with the family?' Cassie observed as her brother pushed open a door and flicked on a light, her voice drained of life, her energy levels on the floor.

Psyching herself up to the point when she could have argued her case with her husband, only to discover he was miles away, had been an anticlimax of near-stupefying proportions.

'No, thank the Lord!' He ushered her through to a sitting room, comfortably furnished with a couple of armchairs, colourful rugs on the polished boards of the floor.

'I guess I deserved every last bit of it, but the way the three old ladies kept watching me, as if they expected me to sneak out with the family silver, was doing my head in. I think Roman knew that. Anyway, he offered me the use of this place.'

Roy crossed to a plain wooden cupboard and produced a bottle of wine, two glasses. Cassie, uncomfortably conscious of forgetting her twin's problems while she wallowed in her own, asked, 'You're settling in?'

'Sure.' He drew the cork. 'Don't hover; park yourself. It's basic but it's comfortable. It's good to have my own space.'

'I meant—' Cassie sank into an armchair, trying not to worry about him '—the work here on the estate, Roman's attitude.'

'He hasn't got one, not like the old ladies. In fact, he's quite a guy when you stop to think about it. I offered to pay back the money I'd borrowed—' He reddened as he saw her eyebrows practically hit the ceiling. 'Right—the money I *took*. Said he could dock some out of my wages each week. But he said no. Provided I toed the line here, the whole thing was forgotten.'

'And are you? Toeing the line?'

For the sake of the tiny new life inside her she refused the glass of wine he offered her, suddenly too weary to ask for a glass of water to ease her dry mouth and throat.

The drive to Sanlucar tonight was out of the question. Apparently Roman could forgive her twin for stealing from him, abusing his trust. Would he forgive her own supposed misdemeanours, believe her when she told him she hadn't committed any?

'Don't worry, sis, I've learnt my lesson,' Roy said quietly, sitting on the low, chunky table in front of her. 'At first I thought I'd hate it here, thought I'd miss the night life, the pretty *señoritas* and fast cars, the fancy restaurants. But you know what? I didn't. I enjoy the work, learning how the estate's managed and that sort of stuff. I'm not going to mess up again or do anything to spoil my opportunities here. Roman as good as promised that if I shape up I can take over when the present manager retires in a few years' time.

'Trouble is—' he spread his hands '—Roman's talking of selling up—everything except the house in Jerez—and taking off. It was a real bombshell, believe me. That's why we were so relieved to see you. You can talk some sense into him.'

Cassie felt the colour drain from her face. 'I don't understand,' she whispered. This vast estate had been in his family for countless generations; he was fiercely proud of his heritage. How could he even think of selling up, denying his future heir his enviable inheritance?

'Nor do the rest of us. I thought you, as his wife, might be able to throw some light on the situation,' he answered soberly. 'There was the reconciliation, the second honeymoon. Then—' He made a slashing movement with one hand. 'He was back here. Alone. Nobody knew what had happened to you. Twenty-four hours later, the aunts scuttled off. Talk about a black mood; nobody dared go near him!

'Then, a few weeks later, he took off. To England, by all accounts. Late the next day he was back here—breathing more thunder, according to Asunción. He told the estate manager he was selling up, then, so gossip has it, got blind drunk, and that's a first as far as anyone here knows.

'This morning he went to Sanlucar. The property there will be the first to go. Perhaps you can fill in some details—like what broke the two of you up this time. Something must have done; everyone thinks so. You must have really rattled his cage!'

She could give him details in plenty, but she wasn't going to. This was between her and her husband. And she would do anything she could to make things right between them.

'I'll do what I can,' she promised, her voice firm now, her resolve strong and her energy flooding back. If he was hurting as badly as his astounding decision to sell up would suggest, then she needed to be with him.

She stood up. Forget resting up, tackling the journey to the coast in the morning. She'd go right now. 'If you'll point me at the bathroom, then fix me a flask of coffee, I'll be on my way.'

'But Cass—it's over a hundred miles. Leave it until the morning.' He looked startled. 'There's no point—'

'If I leave now I'll be there before midnight.' She glanced at her watch, cutting through his common sense objections. She would drive until dawn if she had to.

Nothing was going to keep her away from Roman. Not now, and not in the future.

CHAPTER THIRTEEN

CASSIE made the midnight deadline she'd set herself with half an hour to spare. She parked the hired car in one of the small Moorish squares, grabbed her overnight bag from the passenger seat and straightened up, stretching the kinks out of her spine and shoulders, blinking her eyes as she tried to rid them of the uncomfortably hot and gritty feeling.

The pavement tables outside the café that she and Roman had favoured were still fully occupied. Couples, mostly, enjoying a late supper; people in the south kept late hours. She could hear the sound of guitar music, melancholy and haunting, the counterpoint of soft laughter.

A sudden draining sense of loss and hopelessness swamped her. Would she and Roman ever wander hand in hand down to their favourite café, sit in the shade of the orange tree and watch the world go by, cocooned in a warm and loving relationship?

Or would tonight bring the end of everything?

The square was sheltered from the Atlantic winds and Cassie dragged in a deep, steadying gulp of the soft, dark night air, then headed upwards through the warren of narrow streets, lit by lamps high up on the walls of the jumbled buildings.

She wasn't nervous, she told herself, trying to quiet the manic pitter-patter of her heart. Just keyed-up. Tonight would be a turning point. Could she and Roman at last begin to communicate? They had to if they were to make any sense of the emotional mess they were in!

And she was as much to blame as he was, unable to tell him of her needs, the way she felt, how very deeply she loved him.

The house she had always instinctively been drawn to was in darkness, the many windows over-looking the narrow cobbled street tightly shuttered. It seemed withdrawn, closed in on itself, the usual feeling of welcome absent.

She hated to think of this lovely place, where she and Roman had been so briefly happy, passing into the hands of strangers.

But that wasn't going to happen, she told herself staunchly. She wouldn't be here at all if she didn't think that somehow, if they both opened up, they could work things out.

Thankfully, Manuel hadn't yet locked up for the night, and the huge, ornately carved door swung open at her touch. The hall was in darkness. Feeling for the domed brass switch, she depressed it and the overhead chandelier sprang to glittering life.

The feeling of alienation became stronger, something to dread. Several cardboard boxes filled with books stood at the foot of the stairs.

She swallowed round the hard, painful lump in her throat. Roman was already packing his personal belongings, those books he treasured from the extensive library here, which had been built up over the generations by the Fernandez family.

Somehow she had to stop him.

She called his name but her voice echoed, unanswered, in the silence of the ancient house. She had half expected the housekeeper, or her husband, at least, to emerge from their private quarters at the rear of the building, but no one came.

Biting her lip, she searched the ground-floor rooms. Nothing. Only the few gaps on the library shelves, the open wall safe and the briefcase on the table told her that he was somewhere on the premises.

She was panting slightly when she reached the top of the stairs, her hair coming adrift from the pins that had secured it in a neat pleat at the back of her head. She pushed it away from her face with an impatient hand.

A thin sliver of muted light showed beneath the door of the master bedroom, the room they had shared with such passion, giving of their bodies unreservedly yet keeping the things that really mattered hidden. Openness, trusting each other enough to discuss their feelings, hopes and fears.

Not allowing herself to even think that the coming encounter might have an unhappy outcome for both her and her precious unborn child, she opened the door and walked into the bedroom.

Only the bedside lamp was lit, casting shadows into the corners of the room. Roman was dragging his clothes from the hanging cupboard by the dim light, tossing them haphazardly into an open suitcase.

Hers, the clothes he had insisted on buying her all those weeks ago, were in a pile on the bed. A huge lump formed in her throat.

Without missing a beat, without turning, he said, 'If you've come for your things, you needn't have bothered. Teresa returns tomorrow; I was going to ask her to pack them up and send them on.'

He did turn then, slowly. The light from the lamp picked out his features, emphasising a new and disquieting harshness. He was wearing a white shirt tucked into slate-grey trousers; it made his skin look dark by contrast, his eyes black and unforgiving.

She swallowed convulsively and blurted, trying to lighten the tense atmosphere, 'How did you know it was me? It could have been anyone—a burglar!'

'I knew,' he said, almost uninterestedly. 'And "burglar" fits. You stole something from me, and I don't for a moment think you've come to give it back.'

A mind like a maze didn't come near describing his tortuous thought processes. She'd left here taking only the things she'd brought with her! But now wasn't the time to ask why he was adding theft to the long list of things he'd stacked up against her.

He gave her a last, penetrating look from beneath his brows, his mouth a hard, straight line, then closed the open suitcase with his foot, bent to fasten it and straightened up again.

He was leaving, she thought, panicking, as he

hefted the heavy case and strode towards the door where she was standing. As far as he was concerned she didn't even merit the title of unfinished business.

Her heart gave a violent twist of anguish. It couldn't end liked this—she wouldn't let it!

'We need to talk.' Her voice sounded ragged. Cassie stood her ground, though. If he wanted to go through that door he would have to lift her bodily off her feet. And she was getting the distinct impression that touching her in any way at all was the last thing he wanted to have to do.

'Why?' The question was flat. But he did stop, keeping distance between them, his eyes coldly dismissive.

First things first. Conscious for the first time of her travel-stained clothes, her hair all over the place, her possibly manic appearance, she levelled her voice and told him, 'I was at Las Colinas earlier this evening. Roy said it was common knowledge by now that you intend to sell up. Everything.'

One black brow tilted upwards fractionally. 'And you followed me all the way down here? *Por dios!* you must be eager. For the clothes you left behind? Or were you intending to wheedle your way back into my life via the bedroom? Decided you prefer living in luxury in Spain to sharing a flat with your lover?'

Cassie closed her eyes briefly, her head going back as if to force the threatening tears back right where they came from. She'd expected initial difficulties, but they were turning out to be more painful than she could ever have imagined.

'And not quite everything,' he corrected, loosing his grip on the case, letting it drop to the floor. 'The house in Jerez will stay in the family, for the benefit of the older generation.' He lifted his shoulders in an uncaring shrug. 'After the place has served its purpose, who knows? It will probably go the same way as the estate and this house.'

'You can't do it!' Her throat tightened up again, the words emerging thickly. He would spend the rest of his life regretting it; his heritage was the most important thing in his life.

He crossed his arms across his chest, his long legs straddled, his aristocratic nostrils narrowed. 'No one tells me what I can and cannot do.'

His arrogance pricked her on the raw, despite her compassion. Knowing what his proud heritage meant to him, she knew that something deeply traumatic had forced him to this decision. 'A law unto yourself?' she snapped sardonically. 'What was it you used to say? That you were merely the custodian of your inheritance, honour-bound to hand it on to the next generation in a better state than when it came to you. Or have you conveniently forgotten that?'

She saw a muscle jerk at the side of his mouth, another clench along his hard jawline. 'As there is to be no future generation, I see no point in tying myself to places that hold nothing but bad memories of a woman I don't know any more. I thought I did know you. For a few perfect weeks you had me fooled.'

Her heart lifted. The feeling was so strong it was almost a pain. He had followed her to England to ask her to go back to him, of course he had, and she hadn't lost sight of that. Was it possible that he was feeling as bereft as she was? How could she prove that she loved him, that there had never been anyone else for her?

'Roman—' She wanted to go to him, to hold him, to take the pain away. But even though the hope in her heart was a great and desperate thing, she knew it was too soon. She had to convince him that what he'd seen and heard back at Guy's flat wasn't what it must have seemed.

'Roman.' She repeated his name softly. 'There is a point. You do have an heir.' Unconsciously, her hand rested against her still-flat tummy, then dropped shakily back to her side as she registered the immediate and contemptuous curl of his mouth.

'You try to pass your lover's child off as mine? You insult me, *señora*!'

'The baby is *not* Guy's!'

'Nor mine. You were protected by the contraceptive pill when we were—were together. Or have you, too, very conveniently forgotten you told me that? Do you take me for a fool?' His fists were clenched at his sides, a white line of temper around his mouth. 'I saw you together with my own eyes. Barely dressed. I heard what he said. You were living with him. Well, *señora*, you may go right back to him, with my blessing!'

Shakily, she passed a hand over her burning forehead. This was her worst nightmare. But, unlike a nightmare, she knew she wouldn't wake and leave the horrors behind.

They would stay with her until the end of her days.

Weariness swamped her. It had been a long, long day. The flight out to Jerez, the seemingly endless drive, hither and thither. And nothing accomplished. Zilch. Zero. He would never believe she loved him; more than anything in the world she loved him...

Even if she told him?

She filled her lungs with much needed oxygen. She had to make him believe her. She had to! 'Roman—I always loved you. I've never made love with any other man, despite what you thought. I was able to express my love for you physically because I'd finally grown up, begun to rate myself as a human being—a woman. And I believe—' she dragged in a shaky breath '—that you had finally learned to love me, too.'

She couldn't look at him, couldn't bear to see the cynical disbelief in his eyes which would mean she'd failed. She began to pace the floor, nervous energy overcoming her tiredness, making her restless.

'I'd hoped you'd tell me you wanted me to stay beyond the three months you'd stipulated. Hoped you wanted to make our marriage work as much as I did. But you said I was free to go. I took it that I was no longer any use to you because you'd just heard that Delfina had got herself engaged. What else was I to think?

'Thanks to you, my old flat above Cindy's shop was no longer available. I had nowhere to stay. Guy offered to put me up until I got back on my feet. Against my better judgement, I accepted. I don't know why he said the things he did. Only that—'

'He's in love with you,' Roman injected blankly. 'Unfortunately.'

Silence. She had her back to him; he wasn't responding to her declarations of love. She had opened her heart and he could say nothing in return. Because he thought she was lying?

There was nothing left for her to say except, 'Later, a paternity test can be arranged. It will prove beyond any doubt that you are the father of my child.'

Tears clogged her throat. That it should come down to this. A clinical procedure when, in a perfect world, all it needed was love. And trust.

But this wasn't a perfect world. And very few people in it were free of imperfections.

And still the silence was deafening. He had decided that what he had felt for her wasn't worth the hassle. He could do without her.

But could he do without his child?

The thought of the tiny, precious life within her tore her apart. She pressed her fingertips to her throbbing temples and reached the hardest, most painful decision of her life.

'When you're satisfied that the baby is yours, then

I will hand him or her over to you. To your safe-keeping. Hang on to your heritage for the sake of your heir. I'll—' her voice faltered, the words choking her. But she knew it had to be this way, there wasn't any other.

It would kill her to give up her baby—all the joy in the world would end for her on that dreadful day—but she loved Roman far too much to allow him to be deprived of the child he had always wanted to carry on his name.

'I'll ask only one thing. To be kept...informed...of progress. I'll keep out of the way, never interfere. The occasional photograph... would be welcome.'

CHAPTER FOURTEEN

'CASS.' His voice was harsh. 'Do you know what you're saying?'

He was standing behind her now. Not near enough to touch. But she could feel his warmth, the strength and sheer male vitality of him.

She shuddered convulsively, wanting him to take her in his arms and tell her everything would be all right. Knowing he wouldn't.

'Yes.' It was as much as she could do to get the word out. Her whole body felt as if it were wired to a detonator. Any moment now she could disintegrate, fragment into a million ragged pieces.

'Why?' A heartbeat of silence. Then, 'You do not want our child? You want to be rid of it?' he asked, ice in his voice.

At last he believed the baby was his. Because she'd offered the solution of a paternity test? She folded her arms tightly around her body, trying to hold herself together.

'Of course I want my child! Damn you!' The emotional protestation was torn from her, her voice high and hard, splintering the soft warm air. How could he think that of her? *Why* was he so cruelly intent on thinking the very worst of her?

'Then why would you give your baby away? To me? Cass, I need to know,' he persisted, his voice low, deeper than she had ever heard it.

Her shoulders were held high, rigid with tension, with the effort of keeping herself together. He touched her then, lightly massaging the knots along her collarbone, and the touch of the hands that had brought so much magic into her life for such a brief time was almost her undoing. 'Tell me,' he insisted quietly.

'You—you could give our child a far better quality of life than I ever could,' she said raggedly, wanting to get this over before she broke down completely. 'But that's—that's not the most important consideration.'

Her voice roughened, every word she said seeming to distance her from the new life she carried. 'The dynasty your family founded, the sense of history and pride that you seem intent on throwing away is your child's birthright. Having an heir would stop you from making the greatest mistake of your life— turning your back on your heritage because of the bad memories I made for you. I can't let you do that! Don't you see?'

Reined-in sobs were building up pressure in her chest; it was getting more and more difficult to control the misery that was overwhelming her. 'I know—know you would love our child. Believe me, I wouldn't be doing this if I had any doubts about that.'

Her slight shoulders shook, her hands flying to

cover her face as the pent-up sobs finally escaped. She had made her decision and it had been the hardest thing she'd ever had to do. She'd said what had to be said. The only pity was she hadn't been able to walk away from this traumatic scene with some kind of dignity.

Why couldn't he love her as much as she knew he would love their child? Why had whatever it was he had felt for her turned into bitterness? Why, when he surely must have accepted the truth of what she'd told him—that she had always loved him, that there had never been any other man for her?

He said nothing. By now his very silence told her that the quite obviously tenuous feelings he'd once had for her were now well and truly dead. But he did turn her gently round, enfolding her loosely within the circle of his arms, allowing her head to droop forward against the broad expanse of his chest.

Just as anyone with an ounce of compassion in their make-up would offer brief comfort to another distraught human being. She wouldn't let herself read any more into it than that.

'Cass,' he said moments later, one of his hands straying to her hair, the other still clasped loosely around her waist. 'Enough. Getting rid of tension's all very well. Too much weeping will harm you and our baby.'

That effectively stopped the feeble outpourings, stiffened her spine. Of course. The baby she was carrying would be his prime consideration.

She lifted her head from his thoroughly wettened

shirt, 'I have no intention of harming my baby! So don't worry—getting an heir was the only reason you married me in the first place, other than getting your family off your back. You've won on both counts. Just don't—don't rub it in!'

She wasn't going to cry again. She was not! What was done was done, by her own decree. Now she had to learn to live with it. Somehow.

'Shh. Stop torturing yourself. You will make yourself ill.' He lifted her bodily and carried her to the huge double bed, stacking the pillows carefully behind her, one hand holding her down as she tried to scramble to her feet again.

'Be still,' he commanded gently, and the fight went out of her, utter tiredness seeping into her bones. 'You are quite right,' he told her as she slumped back against the pillows.

Keeping his eyes on her troubled, tear-stained face, he bent over her to remove her shoes, then sat on the edge of the mattress and eased his fingers through her long tousled hair, gently removing the few remaining pins. 'I have won. You stole something from me and now you have brought it back.'

'What?' she demanded truculently. She disliked this new mood of consideration and caring as much as she disliked his earlier stiff silences.

He was only concerned about the baby she'd promised to give over to him. If she hadn't been pregnant he would have probably told her to go jump in the wide waters of the Guadalquiver. 'I've never taken a thing from you—don't mix me up with my twin!'

She didn't want to be here; she wanted to be somewhere else. Somewhere dark and private where she could lick her wounds and try to come to terms with the promise she'd made him.

And she didn't want him to see her in this state; overemotional, her face red and puffy from crying, her hair a mess, the linen jacket and trousers crumpled, spotted with the coffee stains that had resulted from her tussle with the recalcitrant top of the flask Roy had filled for her.

'You stole my happiness,' he told her softly. 'My pride in my heritage—just about everything that made life worthwhile.' He took her hands in his, lifting them to his lips, his kisses as light as butterfly wings on her knuckles. 'And now you have brought it back.' He raised his head, his features solemn. 'And you are right again. I needed an heir. But that was not the reason I married you. I felt this great affection for you, my Cass. I had this huge urge to protect you and care for you. This I had never felt for any other woman. I knew—well, I hoped—that you had a fondness for me, too.

'But sexually, you didn't want to know. It used to tear me apart because at that time I didn't understand it. So I used to absent myself for long periods of time. It was only when you went away that first time that I realised how much I loved you—despite the way our marriage had turned out.'

'My fault!' she blurted miserably, hating her

younger self. She'd been such a timid fool back then.
But was she just as big an idiot now, going out of
her mind, hearing things she so desperately wanted
to hear? Or did he really, truly mean he had once
loved her?

'No!' he countered vehemently. 'Mine entirely.
But we're not going to argue about it. All that's over,
it is—what do you say in your country?—water under the bridge. What matters now is what we make
of our future.'

Cassie bit down on her wobbly lower lip, then
asked bluntly, because she just had to know. 'You
do want me, as well as the baby? You do believe I
have never made love with any other man?'

'Cass—' He drew in a long breath. 'I believe you
implicitly.' His eyes softened. They suddenly looked
suspiciously moist. 'You were willing to make the
biggest sacrifice a woman can make, for my sake,'
he said emotionally. 'That told me how much you
love me; it made my unworthy suspicions ridiculous.
The depth of your love humbles me, *querida*.'

He stood up, his mood changing abruptly. 'You
are exhausted, my Cass. I am going to take very great
care of you. That is my first duty. Tomorrow, I will
make an immediate appointment for you to see an
obstetrician—one of the best. I will, of course, ac-
company you. I will be with you every step of the
way through this pregnancy. But now I will run a
bath, and while you relax in warm water I will make
you hot milk. And you will eat?'

His dark brows furrowed. 'In your mad dash

around the countryside I don't suppose you thought of food,' he accused, planting his feet apart. 'You must take better care of yourself, and if you won't do it, then I must,' he stated firmly. 'Teresa and Manuel don't return until tomorrow—a family birthday celebration. She left me things that are probably too spicy for your condition. You will like a good plain omelette—'

'Stop!' Cassie wriggled round onto her knees, her eyes wet with emotional tears, her mouth curving in a tender smile. Roman had never looked or sounded so utterly Spanish as he did at this moment. And so determined to get things right.

'Pamper me if you must—I'm not complaining! But eating's low on my list of priorities at the moment.' She held out her hands to him. 'Forget your duty, just for a minute, and come and talk to me. Tell me, did you mean it—about realising you really did love me when—?'

'When you left me. I was utterly shattered. I couldn't believe how empty I felt.' He sucked in his lower lip, and it was the first time she had seen him appear indecisive. 'You are sure you are up to more talk?'

He capitulated gladly at her bright-eyed nod and moved back towards her, his own eyes soft as he took her outstretched hands in his. 'My instinct was to drag you back, so that we could sit down together, somewhere away from my family, and try to find out what had turned our marriage into a disaster zone.'

Sitting on the side of the bed, he held her hands

against his chest. 'But the sensible side of me said that would be wrong. From what I knew of your past, and my misguided handling of you during our marriage, all your life you'd been told what to do, pushed into being what other people wanted you to be. You needed time to get to know yourself.'

He smiled gently into her bright, tear-spangled eyes. 'I kept a watching brief—and one day I'll tell you how I did this—and told myself to be patient for one year. Then I would come for you, and bring you flowers and perfume and jewels. And my love. And woo my bride back to me.'

'But I came to you first,' she murmured thoughtfully.

If Roy hadn't stolen that money, she wouldn't have gone to Roman; he would have come to her. To woo her back to him. She wouldn't have been able to resist him, she knew she wouldn't, because he had always been all she had ever wanted. So much misery would have been avoided.

'That was when the sensible part of me went on holiday.' He leant over and kissed the end of her nose. 'I'd expected to see a change in you, but the extent of it took me by surprise. You'd regained all that lost weight, lost the haunted look that used to worry me so much—you had poise, confidence. You did not look like a woman who would be easily wooed—not unless you wanted to be, and I was sure at that stage that you did not. So I got this crazy idea of using blackmail and later deeply regretted it. It was so unworthy.'

Cassie wriggled forward, snuggling into his side. She was home; she and her baby were loved and wanted. 'Which was why,' she said, smothering a yawn, 'you were so stiff and proper when you told me I was free to go. I thought—'

'I know what you thought,' he said gravely. 'But you couldn't have been further from the truth. I had to give you the choice—no pressure. I wanted, with all my heart, to hear you say you wanted to stay with me. And now I know you will.'

'Always,' she responded sleepily, her bright head drooping into the hollow of his shoulder. 'Tell me you love me.'

'I love you.' She heard the smile in his voice. 'So much so, I knew I had to go far away from memories if I wanted to stay sane,' he murmured against her hair. 'Now all that is over—and for you,' he went on briskly, 'bath, bed and food.'

He lifted her effortlessly and she looped her arms around his neck. 'No food. It's very late and I'm too sleepy to eat.' The truth was, she didn't want to let him out of her sight. If she did, she would begin to think this was all a dream.

She gave an enormous yawn to prove her point and he shot her a frowning look of concern as he flicked on the light in the *en suite* and slid her down the length of his body, steadying her with one hand, turning on the taps to fill the bath with the other.

The water gushing, steam misting the marble walls, he slid her crumpled jacket from her shoulders, revealing the pretty lace bra that barely constrained her full, creamy breasts. She heard the rough, urgent tug of his breath and smiled softly as she suggested huskily, 'Why don't you join me?'

'Believe me—' he ran a finger slowly down the inviting indentation of her cleavage '—there is nothing in the world I would enjoy more.' There were pinpoints of searing light in the smoky depths of his eyes and a wry smile tugged at the corners of his long, sensual mouth as he added dryly, 'But it would be a very bad idea. You need to rest. One thing would lead to another and neither of us would get any sleep at all, you understand me?'

Only too well, she thought, already swaying on her feet as he turned off the taps and tested the water. But it would have been heavenly…

Cassie stirred lazily beneath the soft covers. It was dawn. A new day. A new beginning. A contented smile curved her soft lips.

She could only dimly remember climbing out of the scented bath water, Roman stepping forward to smother her in a huge towel, gently patting her dry.

Her overnight bag was still in the hall. It had seemed too much effort to ask him to bring it to her. Besides, he had gathered her into his arms and slid her, boneless and naked, between the silky sheets…

And now he slept beside her, his tough features relaxed and almost vulnerable, his soft dark hair rumpled, his jaw darkly stubbled. Her heart lurched with tenderness as she stretched out a hand to touch him.

He, too, was naked. Her smile was wicked now,

her amber eyes glinting as she wriggled closer and wrapped her arms around him, glorying in the sensation of loving and being loved in return.

She felt his lithe body stir, as if her touch had brought him immediately awake. And then he turned, pulling her close before lifting himself on one elbow, his face only inches from hers, his eyes soft, liquid silver, as he asked, 'You are feeling good now?'

'Mmm,' she murmured, wriggling closer, her breath snagging as she felt his hard response against the softness of her tummy. 'But I could feel better.'

'How?' His brows peaked, emphasising the line between them, and she put her hand against the side of his face, the rough dark texture sparking tremors of electric sensation deep inside her.

'This—' She rubbed the ball of her thumb across the carved sensuality of his mouth, then claimed it with her own, and his answering kiss was deeper, more tender than she had ever known it, touching her soul, claiming it, making it his own.

'Cassie,' he said raggedly when lack of breath parted them, 'I adore you.' He pushed his fingers through her hair, dark colour suffusing the skin along his taut cheekbones. 'I want you so badly. But is that all right for you, and for the baby? If I am slow? And careful?'

'Well...' she said consideringly, smoothing her hands over his shoulders and then down his chest to the tautness of his stomach. 'Slow and careful? I don't believe we've done that before.' Her eyes glinted wickedly into his as her hands slid between his thighs. 'Let's see how it works out, shall we?'

'Delicious,' she husked an hour later. 'Divine, pure ecstasy.' Her arms lay above her head, their legs tangled together, supine and sated.

Roman shifted on to one shoulder and bent his head to her breasts, burying it between their lushness. 'For me, it was heaven. You are heaven.' A hand strayed to her tummy, fingers rubbing through the tangle of springy curls just below. 'Cassie, *amada*, when did you know we were having a child?' he queried softly, his head lifting, his eyes intent on what his fingers were doing, the way her creamy thighs immediately parted for him.

She told him, her breath coming faster. How could this be happening again, so soon after the last mind-blowing hour?

'And you kept it secret. Why, Cassie *mia*?'

'I wanted to be sure—' Oh, dear heaven, what was he doing? It was almost too much pleasure! 'Be sure you wanted me for me, not because I was to be the mother of your child.'

'Then I think,' he said with a decided glint in his eyes, 'that it is my pleasant duty to reassure you.'

And he proceeded to do exactly that.

Nine months later.

Three-month-old Sebastian Roman Fernandez looked adorable in his white lace christening robes.

He'd inherited his golden eyes from his mother, but the rest of him was pure Roman.

The family party was going with a swing. Teresa, now Cassie's staunch admirer, had coped magnificently with the preparations, and the guests were spilling out into the courtyard.

The aunts had pronounced Sebastian the most beautiful baby in the whole of Spain, and Doña Elvira had admitted, 'You have made my son happy. I didn't believe you could but you have proved me wrong. My dear, you are a most welcome addition to the family.'

Cassie, her figure restored to normal—apart from a greater fullness in the bosom area which Roman vowed he adored—was dressed in a sleek cream silk shift, the pearls her husband had presented her with on the birth of their son around her elegant neck, her chestnut hair upswept to show them off.

The photographs had been taken and she'd socialised with all of the guests. Now she had gravitated back to the crib, watching her baby son sleep, with love-drenched eyes.

'To the three of us.' Roman joined her, looking incredibly handsome in his lightweight handcrafted suit. He handed her a champagne flute and touched his glass to hers. 'To my beautiful wife, my handsome son, and the happiest, proudest husband and father alive.'

Her smile was radiant as she reached up to put a kiss on the side of his gorgeous mouth, 'I missed you. Where have you been?'

'Talking to Roy. I managed to prise him away from Consuela for long enough to discuss a few projects with him, get his opinions.' His grin was disarming.

'Do you think it's serious—I mean between him and Consuela?'

Her brother and the dark-haired pretty youngest daughter of the estate manager had been inseparable. Cassie could see the attraction between them.

Roy had matured out of all recognition. Deeply tanned, his features tougher and more serious, her brother had turned into one hunky man, the hard work around the estate broadening his shoulders and narrowing a waistline that had formerly tended to bulge.

'Could be,' Roman confirmed. 'In fact, I think it definitely is. And the way Roy's shaping up, he'll step into the job of manager when Miguel retires. And, Cass—' he slipped an arm around her shoulders. '—how would you feel about visiting Las Colinas for a few weeks, introducing young Seb around the place? I know how you love Sanlucar, and this house will always be our permanent home, but—'

'But you yearn for the wide open spaces? You want to poke your long nose in?' Her eyes sparkled for him. 'That's fine by me.'

Where Roman was she would always want to be. He successfully ran his many other businesses from Sanlucar, visiting Seville occasionally for a few hours, but Las Colinas was in his blood.

'You're sure?' He held her eyes. These days they kept nothing from each other; they were almost like one person—with infinitely exciting differences, he had to concede. 'The aunts and my mother could be tactfully moved to Jerez for the length of our stay,' he suggested.

But Cassie shook her head. 'I'm perfectly happy to share space with them. They won't criticise the mother of your heir!'

His smile was wicked. 'No, I don't think they'd dare! Well, if you're happy with that?'

'Happy, full-stop.' She slipped a hand into his and raised her glass. 'To the three of us.' She tilted her head, her smile enigmatic. 'How about four? The heir needs at least one brother or sister to stop him being disgracefully spoiled.'

'Your wish is my command,' he said, his fingers tightening around hers, his smile sleepy and utterly fascinating. 'Mind you,' he added, the incandescence of her answering smile making his heart leap crazily, 'as commands go, I can't think of anything I'd rather put more effort into.'

LONG, TALL TEXANS

EMMETT, REGAN & BURKE

New York Times
extended list bestselling author

Diana PALMER

returns to Jacobsville, Texas, in this special collection featuring rugged heroes, spirited heroines and passionate love stories told in her own inimitable way!

Coming in May 2001 only from Silhouette Books!

Where love comes alive™

Visit Silhouette at www.eHarlequin.com   PSLLT

Harlequin truly does make any time special. . . . This year we are celebrating weddings in style!

A Walk Down the Aisle
WEDDING CELEBRATION

To help us celebrate, we want you to tell us how wearing the Harlequin wedding gown will make your wedding day special. As the grand prize, Harlequin will offer one lucky bride the chance to **"Walk Down the Aisle"** in the Harlequin wedding gown!

There's more...

For her honeymoon, she and her groom will spend five nights at the **Hyatt Regency Maui.** As part of this five-night honeymoon at the hotel renowned for its romantic attractions, the couple will enjoy a candlelit dinner for two in Swan Court, a sunset sail on the hotel's catamaran, and duet spa treatments.

A HYATT RESORT AND SPA

Maui • Molokai • Lanai

To enter, please write, in, 250 words or less, how wearing the Harlequin wedding gown will make your wedding day special. The entry will be judged based on its emotionally compelling nature, its originality and creativity, and its sincerity. This contest is open to Canadian and U.S. residents only and to those who are 18 years of age and older. There is no purchase necessary to enter. Void where prohibited. See further contest rules attached. Please send your entry to:

Walk Down the Aisle Contest

In Canada	In U.S.A.
P.O. Box 637	P.O. Box 9076
Fort Erie, Ontario	3010 Walden Ave.
L2A 5X3	Buffalo, NY 14269-9076

You can also enter by visiting www.eHarlequin.com
Win the Harlequin wedding gown and the vacation of a lifetime!
The deadline for entries is October 1, 2001.

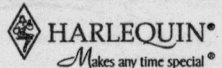

HARLEQUIN®
Makes any time special ®

PHWDACONT1

HARLEQUIN WALK DOWN THE AISLE TO MAUI CONTEST 1197
OFFICIAL RULES
NO PURCHASE NECESSARY TO ENTER

. To enter, follow directions published in the offer to which you are responding. Contest begins April 2, 2001, and ends on October 1, 2001. Method of entry may vary. Mailed entries must be postmarked by October 1, 2001, and received by October 8, 2001.

. Contest entry may be, at times, presented via the Internet, but will be restricted solely to residents of certain geographic areas that are disclosed on the Web site. To enter via the Internet, if permissible, access the Harlequin Web site (www.eHarlequin.com) and follow the directions displayed online. Online entries must be received by 11:59 p.m. E.S.T. on October 1, 2001.

In lieu of submitting an entry online, enter by mail by hand-printing (or typing) on an 8½" x 11" plain piece of paper, your name, address (including zip code), Contest number/name and in 250 words or fewer, why winning a Harlequin wedding dress would make your wedding day special. Mail via first-class mail to: Harlequin Walk Down the Aisle Contest 1197, (in the U.S.) P.O. Box 9076, 3010 Walden Avenue, Buffalo, NY 14269-9076, (in Canada) P.O. Box 637, Fort Erie, Ontario L2A 5X3, Canada.

Limit one entry per person, household address and e-mail address. Online and/or mailed entries received from persons residing in geographic areas in which Internet entry is not permissible will be disqualified.

. Contests will be judged by a panel of members of the Harlequin editorial, marketing and public relations staff based on the following criteria:

- Originality and Creativity—50%
- Emotionally Compelling—25%
- Sincerity—25%

In the event of a tie, duplicate prizes will be awarded. Decisions of the judges are final.

All entries become the property of Torstar Corp. and will not be returned. No responsibility is assumed for lost, late, illegible, incomplete, inaccurate, nondelivered or misdirected mail or misdirected e-mail, for technical, hardware or software failures of any kind, lost or unavailable network connections, or failed, incomplete, garbled or delayed computer transmission or any human error which may occur in the receipt or processing of the entries in this Contest.

Contest open only to residents of the U.S. (except Puerto Rico) and Canada, who are 18 years of age or older, and is void wherever prohibited by law; all applicable laws and regulations apply. Any litigation within the Province of Quebec respecting the conduct or organization of a publicity contest may be submitted to the Régie des alcools, des courses et des jeux for a ruling. Any litigation respecting the awarding of a prize may be submitted to the Régie des alcools, des courses et des jeux only for the purpose of helping the parties reach a settlement. Employees and immediate family members of Torstar Corp. and D. L. Blair, Inc., their affiliates, subsidiaries and all other agencies, entities and persons connected with the use, marketing or conduct of this Contest are not eligible to enter. Taxes on prizes are the sole responsibility of winners. Acceptance of any prize offered constitutes permission to use winner's name, photograph or other likeness for the purposes of advertising, trade and promotion on behalf of Torstar Corp., its affiliates and subsidiaries without further compensation to the winner, unless prohibited by law.

Winners will be determined no later than November 15, 2001, and will be notified by mail. Winners will be required to sign and return an Affidavit of Eligibility form within 15 days after winner notification. Noncompliance within that time period may result in disqualification and an alternative winner may be selected. Winners of trip must execute a Release of Liability prior to ticketing and must possess required travel documents (e.g. passport, photo ID) where applicable. Trip must be completed by November 2002. No substitution of prize permitted by winner. Torstar Corp. and D. L. Blair, Inc., their parents, affiliates, and subsidiaries are not responsible for errors in printing or electronic presentation of Contest, entries and/or game pieces. In the event of printing or other errors which may result in unintended prize values or duplication of prizes, all affected game pieces or entries shall be null and void. If for any reason the Internet portion of the Contest is not capable of running as planned, including infection by computer virus, bugs, tampering, unauthorized intervention, fraud, technical failures, or any other causes beyond the control of Torstar Corp. which corrupt or affect the administration, secrecy, fairness, integrity or proper conduct of the Contest, Torstar Corp. reserves the right, at its sole discretion, to disqualify any individual who tampers with the entry process and to cancel, terminate, modify or suspend the Contest or the Internet portion thereof. In the event of a dispute regarding an online entry, the entry will be deemed submitted by the authorized holder of the e-mail account submitted at the time of entry. Authorized account holder is defined as the natural person who is assigned to an e-mail address by an Internet access provider, online service provider or other organization that is responsible for arranging e-mail address for the domain associated with the submitted e-mail address. **Purchase or acceptance of a product offer does not improve your chances of winning.**

Prizes: (1) Grand Prize—A Harlequin wedding dress (approximate retail value: $3,500) and a 5-night/6-day honeymoon trip to Maui, HI, including round-trip air transportation provided by Maui Visitors Bureau from Los Angeles International Airport (winner is responsible for transportation to and from Los Angeles International Airport) and a Harlequin Romance Package, including hotel accomodations (double occupancy) at the Hyatt Regency Maui Resort and Spa, dinner for (2) two at Swan Court, a sunset sail on Kiele V and a spa treatment for the winner (approximate retail value, $4,000); (5) Five runner-up prizes of a $1000 gift certificate to selected retail outlets to be determined by Sponsor (retail value $1000 ea.). Prizes consist of only those items listed as part of the prize. Limit one prize per person. All prizes are valued in U.S. currency.

For a list of winners (available after December 17, 2001) send a self-addressed, stamped envelope to: Harlequin Walk Down the Aisle Contest 1197 Winners, P.O. Box 4200 Blair, NE 68009-4200 or you may access the www.eHarlequin.com Web site through January 15, 2002.

ntest sponsored by Torstar Corp., P.O. Box 9042, Buffalo, NY 14269-9042, U.S.A.

PHWDACONT2